"Newborn pictures are the best," Frankie explained.

Spence needed a moment. Swallowing, he waited for his heart to sink back into place from where it had lodged in his throat. These were his daughters when they were just a day, maybe hours, old!

"I think they're beautiful."

"I might have extra copies stored in a drawer I can give you along with the thumb drives."

He nodded, not trusting himself to speak.

"I wish I'd been there," Spence said without thinking and realized with a start how much he really did wish it.

Frankie turned her face to his, and tears shone in her eyes. "This is harder than I thought it would be."

"Aw, honey. Don't cry."

Spence put an arm around her and she angled her body toward him and lifted her chin—something she'd done when they were dating and she wanted him to kiss her.

Wait. Take a breath. Think.

He had to be mistaken, right? Then again, not all old habits were bad, were they?

The Cowboy's Twin Surprise

CATHY McDAVID

First Published in Great Britain 2017
By Mills & Boon, an imprint of HarperCollins*Publishers*
1 London Bridge Street, London, SE1 9GF

Large Print edition 2017

© 2017 Cathy McDavid

ISBN: 978-0-263-07189-4

Printed and bound in Great Britain
by CPI Antony Rowe, Chippenham, Wiltshire

Since 2006, *New York Times* bestselling author **Cathy McDavid** has been happily penning contemporary Westerns for Mills & Boon. Every day, she gets to write about handsome cowboys riding the range or busting a bronc. It's a tough job, but she's willing to make the sacrifice. Cathy shares her Arizona home with her own real-life sweetheart and a trio of odd pets. Her grown twins have left to embark on lives of their own, and she couldn't be prouder of their accomplishments.

To Clay and Caitlin,
my own grown twins who will
forever be my little babies—XXOO

Chapter One

"When are you going to quit this job and run away with me?"

The man, seventy if he was a day, stared up at Frankie Hartman with an endearing smile.

She refilled his mug from the pot that was never far away and always contained freshly brewed coffee. Propping an elbow on the counter, she said, "Now, Everett. What about my girls? They're just three. I couldn't possibly leave them."

"Ah. The twins. I forgot."

He hadn't. Everett passed through southern

Arizona at least twice a month, hauling gravel and sand for a regional supplier. The Cowboy Up Café, where Frankie worked her tail off as head waitress, was a regular stop for him and he often engaged her in a flirtatious exchange that both of them knew would lead nowhere.

She didn't mind. Everett was a good tipper. He was also funny and a lot smarter than his good ol' boy appearance and personality would have people think.

In that regard, he wasn't unlike Spence, the errant father of Frankie's twin daughters. But she refused to think about him. Not today. She had much more important matters on her mind.

Tia Maria, owner and manager of the café, would be assembling the staff at any moment and announcing the name of the new manager. Though Tia Maria had dropped only occasional vague hints, Frankie was one hundred percent convinced she'd get the promotion.

Who else? Besides having the most seniority, she'd covered for Tia Maria off and on this past year during the café owner's increasing absences. While Tia Maria wasn't seriously ill, advancing age and health issues had begun to take their toll, and she'd decided to finally retire.

Frankie had been mentally spending the increased salary that came with the promotion for weeks now. Between two young daughters and the house she'd recently purchased, her budget was stretched to its limit.

"Maybe before my next run, you'll reconsider." Everett wasn't ready to give up.

Frankie flashed him the smile she reserved for her favorite customers. "Anything's possible."

She hurried to the pass-through window, grabbed her order and delivered it to the waiting customers. Because the café was shorthanded today, she'd been filling in wherever needed, covering the counter more than the dining area. In between, she watched the door for Tia Maria's return and counted the minutes.

From the corner of her eye, Frankie caught sight of her two younger sisters, Mel and Ronnie. At four months pregnant, Mel had recently started showing and switched from wearing her standard jeans and tucked-in work shirt to stretchy pants and loose tops. She looked both different and adorable.

Waving hello, the pair slipped into a recently vacated booth.

Frankie informed her nearest coworker she was taking a break. She then prepared Mel's favorite herbal tea and a hot chocolate for Ronnie. With luck, they'd be celebrating Frankie's promotion.

"You came." She placed the mugs in front of her sisters. Since Tia Maria frowned on employees sitting at tables with customers, Frankie stood. It was actually a practice she supported.

"Dad and Dolores send their apologies," Mel said.

"No problem."

Frankie hadn't expected either her father or stepmom to show. Cattle buyers were visiting The Small Change Ranch this morning, where her father worked as foreman, and her stepmom lay in bed, recovering from a minor surgical procedure.

Of course, Frankie would love to have all her family here to share in her moment of excitement, but she understood why it wasn't possible.

"Is Sam home with the girls?" Ronnie asked.

"She's picking them up after preschool and bringing them by for a dish of ice cream."

"Did she tell you she's competing at the Camp Verde Rodeo this weekend?"

Frankie sighed. "I swear, I hardly see her anymore."

They'd recently connected with their unknown teenaged sister—when she'd crashed their father's birthday party and demanded a share of his lottery winnings. While accepting of Sam, Mel and Ronnie still had their ups and downs with her, struggling to come to terms with her sudden appearance, her decision to say in Mustang Valley, and the fact their father had had a child with another woman and never told anyone.

Frankie, however, had taken instantly to the

eighteen-year-old, who stayed with her when she wasn't on the road and fit in as if they'd been together their entire lives.

"When's the announcement?" Ronnie blew on and then sipped her hot chocolate.

"Any minute. Whenever Tia Maria gets back." Frankie glanced around, noting the new busboy hadn't cleared two of the tables. "She'd better hurry. We're going to get busy soon."

Though customers continued to come and go, the crowd had thinned during the typical lull between breakfast and lunch. Frankie didn't worry. The well-trained staff, with the exception of the new busboy, would handle the few new customers straggling in.

"Are you nervous?"

Frankie beamed down at Mel. "I'm excited. I can't wait. I have so many ideas for this place."

Had she really been employed at the café fourteen years? She could remember ditching school one afternoon during her junior year to interview with Tia Maria, who, with her steel-colored hair, sharp features and vivid red lipstick, had scared the pants off Frankie. Truth be told, she still did once in a while.

"Will you be able to keep up with the catering after the promotion?"

Mel's question was one Frankie had pondered endlessly since Tia Maria first mentioned retiring.

"If work gets too demanding, I'll just cut back on the catering. Limit myself to friends and family. And the really high-paying jobs, of course."

"How's your crowd-funding campaign coming along?" Ronnie asked.

"I've only raised a few hundred dollars so far." Hardly enough to launch a business, even a side one.

"No one makes better barbecue brisket and ribs than you," Mel added. "Even that place the *New Times* voted number one doesn't compare."

Frankie unabashedly agreed. "But side jobs don't provide company benefits. I need the employer-paid health insurance and vacation days."

They chatted a couple more minutes, until

Frankie noticed the new busboy had yet to clear the two tables. This wasn't the time for her to fall behind in her duties, not with a promotion nearly clinched.

"I'd better get going."

"We're rooting for you, sis."

She hurried off, still not understanding why Tia Maria hadn't simply given her the promotion. What was with all this big announcement stuff?

Frankie located the busboy in the storeroom, hanging out with the assistant cook, and hurriedly dispatched him to the dining area. She then admonished the assistant cook, a notorious flirt who was much too old for the kid, before returning to the counter, where customers were waiting for either refills, their check, to place their order or be served.

At least three new people had arrived. She summed them up in a flash. A middle-aged couple—tourists judging by their cargo shorts and T-shirts—and a young cowboy, probably in his early thirties, though it was hard to tell from this angle.

Frankie delivered an order of pancakes, and then snatched the coffeepot from the warming plate, ready to offer the cowboy and middle-aged couple a steaming mug. At that moment, the cowboy turned from talking to Everett and looked directly at her.

He wore an enormous grin, and his green-gray eyes danced with amusement.

Frankie froze as if hit with a stun gun. Only her heart moved, and it beat hard enough to crack a rib.

No, no, no! This could not be happening.

She closed her eyes. When she opened them, Spencer Bohanan still sat there, acting as if he hadn't been gone for over four years and without so much as a phone call. A text. An e-mail. A greeting passed on from a mutual friend.

"What are you doing here?" she demanded, storming over to him.

"Now, now, honey."

Honey! Frankie came unglued. Who did he think he was?

"I'm busy, Spence."

"Cook still making those special hash browns with the green peppers and onions?"

"I don't have time for this."

Her legs started to shake, knocking together at the knees. Worse, Tia Maria had just entered the front door, accompanied by a well-dressed man Frankie hadn't seen before. She needed to get Spence out of there.

"I'll have the two-egg special, over easy with wheat toast and a side of the special hash browns." Turning his coffee mug right side up, he said, "Seeing as you have the pot, I'll take a shot."

She wanted to strangle him for too many reasons to count. Not the least of which was the last time he'd left, he'd given her all of fifteen hours' warning. She'd told him to stay away for good. To never come back. Find someone new who could tolerate his wandering ways.

And, he had. The first two, anyway. Maybe the third. She hadn't inquired.

Everett didn't bother hiding his stare. Frankie sought out her sisters, who looked on with slack-jawed wonder. Probably half the café customers were observing Frankie and Spence. Those who knew their history were relaying it to their neighbors in hushed whispers. If Frankie strained, she swore she could hear them.

"Sweethearts since high school."

"He'd leave for some rodeo or ranch job, then appear on her doorstep six months later."

"She always took him back. Well, except for that last time. Heard they had a lulu of a fight."

"Do you think he's the father of her girls?"

"She refuses to say who is, but my money's on him."

"Does he know?"

"If not, he will soon enough. No one keeps a secret in this town."

That last statement—imagined or real—sent Frankie into a state of panic. Coffee sloshed out of the pot and landed on her shoe, the result of her unsteady grip.

"You need to go. Now," she muttered between clenched teeth.

Spence's grin didn't waver. "Can we talk first?"

He'd heard about the girls! She should leave for the preschool this very instant, not wait for Sam. At the least, she needed to call her youngest sister and warn her to...what? Pack the girls' clothes so that Frankie could whisk them away?

"I owe you an apology," Spence said, his tone sounding contrite in that boyish way of his. "More than one. I'd like the chance to issue them. That's all."

Okay. Perhaps he didn't know. Frankie's head swam. This was confusing. And alarming. She'd considered telling him about the girls a thousand times, always talking herself out of it before placing the call.

Was fate giving her a push, reminding her of all the good reasons she should inform Spence he was a father? Only one way to find out.

"I'm off at three," she said.

"I just so happen to be free at three. I'll pick you up."

"No way. I'll meet you. Six o'clock at the park." *And don't talk to anyone in town between now and then.*

His face lit with the same smile she remembered from high school, when they'd been assigned as lab partners in chemistry class, and he'd stolen her heart. He'd yet to return it, even to this day. In her weaker moments, she admitted she had yet to reclaim it.

Frankie started to speak, only to be cut off by the busboy tapping her on the shoulder.

"Tia Maria says for everyone to meet her in the office."

The moment was here. The announcement naming her the new manager. Struggling to control the myriad emotions whirling around inside her, she shakily poured Spence's coffee.

"Stay out of trouble," she warned him before following the busboy, remembering at the last second to return the pot to the warmer.

"I'll be waiting for you," Spence called after her, laughter in his voice.

Frankie balled her hands into fists. He would have to be every bit as good-looking as always. Tall, broad-shouldered, and perfectly proportioned in all the right places.

"A little advance notice would have been nice," she grumbled to herself while untying her apron. She refused to be wearing an orange juice stain the size of a saucer when she accepted her promotion.

THE ENTIRE STAFF on duty, including the cook, had gathered in the area outside the manager's office. Standing beside Tia Maria was the well-dressed man Frankie had noticed earlier. Who was he, and why was he there?

The café owner's wrinkled face glowed as her glance encompassed everyone there. "I'll make this short. I don't want to keep the customers waiting."

Frankie's stomach churned. Damn Spence for showing up today of all days. She needed to be on her toes. Ready and alert. Not distracted by the thought of him sitting there.

Tia Maria's gaze fell on Frankie, who went still. After a brief pause, it continued to the next person. "As you know, I'm retiring at the end of the month, and I promised to announce the new manager today."

Frankie twisted the apron between her suddenly sweaty hands.

Tia Maria took the man's arm and nudged him forward. "This is my nephew, Antonio. He moved from Las Cruces to take over for me. I'm very pleased the Cowboy Up Café will remain in the family."

Frankie went numb all over as seven heads instantly swiveled in her direction. They'd all expected her to get the promotion, too.

She reached for the wall, feeling slightly unbalanced.

"I'm sorry," someone near her murmured.

"Me, too." Had she said that out loud? Her mouth didn't seem to be working correctly. "Damn."

She definitely said *that* out loud, though softly. She'd been counting on the promotion and the raise. She deserved it, after all her years of loyal service. For Tia Maria to bring in a family member without telling Frankie was unfair. Not to mention total nepotism.

Drawing in a breath, she straightened her spine, acutely aware of the stares aimed at her.

"Congratulations and welcome," she said, with as much dignity and calm as she could muster. Then she spun on her heels, not caring if she received a reprimand later. She simply would not cry in front of these people.

Entering the dining area, she fully intended to bury herself in work as a defense against her acute disappointment. Naturally, the first person she noticed was Spence. He'd left the counter in order to join her sisters at their table. Of all the nerve!

Had they called him over? It was possible—Frankie's entire family had always liked Spence. She didn't worry that her sisters would say anything about the girls. Mel and Ronnie were completely trustworthy in that regard. So what were they talking about, with their heads bent together over the table? Frankie squinted. Was that his phone they were staring at?

Pictures. Had to be. Spence's family had moved from Mustang Valley years ago. He was probably updating her sisters on the Bohanan doings. Their laughter floated across the room and grated on Frankie's nerves.

It occurred to her that she'd completely forgotten to turn in his breakfast order. She did that now, rather than break her bad news to her sisters in front of him. They caught sight of her and gestured her over. She pretended not to see them.

One by one, the staff returned to their stations, unusually subdued. Frankie accepted a "Tough break" from Cook and an "I don't know what she's thinking" from one of the waitresses. Neither remark lifted her spirits. Worse, tears stung her eyes.

She sneaked off to the restroom, not caring about the customers or Tia Maria's potential anger. Frankie needed a moment alone. Five minutes later, she felt strong enough to face the world again. On her way out of the restroom, she ran into Mel.

"I'm shocked," her sister gushed. "Do you believe he's here? Are you going to tell him about the girls?"

"Maybe. Yes. Probably."

"Really? Jeez, Frankie. Are you ready?"

"We're meeting at six. The park. Neutral territory."

A customer emerged from the men's room and gave them a nod as he passed.

Mel lowered her voice. "What will you say? I mean, you can't just blurt out, 'Hey, you're a dad.'"

"I'm not sure."

"You'd better hurry. Someone will say something if they haven't already."

"I know, I know."

Mel's demeanor abruptly changed. Grabbing her by both arms, she broke into a happy smile. "So, when do you officially start?"

Frankie had trouble forming the words. Before she could get any out, Tia Maria poked her head around the corner and crooked a finger at her. *Uh-oh.* She'd been caught slacking off.

"Call you later," she told Mel, and didn't wait for a reply.

Her employer led her to the same spot where the staff meeting had taken place moments ago. Frankie wondered if she was about to be fired. Could this day get any worse?

"I should have told you about hiring my nephew," the older woman said, a trace of contrition in her voice. "I realize you expected to get the job."

"You did imply as much." Frankie resisted the anger building inside her.

"I was considering you, I swear. Then my sister mentioned my nephew was looking for a job. He's a good man. Honest and trustworthy."

And Frankie wasn't?

"I really do want to keep the restaurant in the family," Tia Maria continued.

"Does he have any experience?"

"Some. I'm hoping you'll teach him."

Frankie took that to mean the man knew nothing of the restaurant business. She started to speak when her cell phone vibrated from inside her pocket, signaling she had a message. Was Sam texting about the girls? Frankie had trouble concentrating.

"I thought that you could help with the ordering and inventorying," Tia Maria said. "You and Antonio can learn together."

No one had ever been allowed to assist with, much less take over, this task handled by the café owner. She was throwing Frankie a bone.

"Does it come with a raise?"

Tia Maria drew back. "The experience will be very valuable."

For what? Frankie would never need it here. Unless Tia Maria was expecting her to quit. Was it possible?

"A raise would be better," she said.

Tia Maria relented with a shrug. "I'll consider it."

If only Frankie could quit. But she needed a

regular salary to cover the bills and put food on the table. Besides, there weren't many well-paying opportunities for a waitress in Mustang Valley other than the café.

"*Por favor*, do your best to make my Antonio feel welcomed. Moving away from home is going to be a big adjustment for him."

Frankie had a few big adjustments of her own waiting for her, one of them named Spence. "Sure. No problem."

For the first time, Tia Maria smiled. And why not? She'd gotten her way. Her nephew was now manager of the café, and Frankie had basically agreed to train him without guaranteed compensation. She could kick herself.

Well, she'd just have to expand her catering business. Realistically, she had no other choice if she hoped to increase her earning potential. At the moment, being her own boss sounded very appealing.

Before returning to the counter, she paused at the doorway to quickly check her phone—

a practice generally frowned on, but Frankie didn't care.

All right, not a text. Rather, an e-mail from her crowd-funding campaign, notifying her of a donation. Must be the universe telling her she was right to concentrate on her own business rather than someone else's.

Tapping the phone's screen, she opened the e-mail and followed the link to the donation page. Blinking, she looked again. Then a third time. Something wasn't right. There must be a mistake. The amount showing was a whopping ten thousand dollars!

She reread the notification over and over, closed the link and started again. The amount in big green numbers remained the same. A numeral one followed by lots of zeros. Ten freakin' thousand dollars.

Who would contribute that kind of money to her fledgling catering business? Using her fingers, she expanded the screen to better read the name. Spencer Bohanan! No flipping way.

She was going to strangle him. No, wait. First

she was going to give him a piece of her very angry mind, then strangle him. How dare he? This wasn't the least bit funny. In fact, it was mean. A terrible, humorless, tasteless joke.

Not caring about Tia Maria or the new manager/nephew or even her job, she marched over to the table where Spence still sat with her sisters.

Shoving her phone in his face, she stated, "I'm not amused."

He leaned back to put more than two inches between himself and the phone and read the screen. "Wow. That came through fast."

"What are you thinking?"

"I'm contributing to your catering business." He grinned. "Isn't that the point of a crowd-funding campaign?"

Frankie paid no attention to her sisters, who watched slack-jawed as if witnessing an impending catastrophe. "You don't have ten thousand dollars."

"The donation wouldn't have gone through if I didn't."

Wha… Wait. That was true. Frankie remembered reading the terms and conditions. All donations were guaranteed by credit card or an online payment system. Spence couldn't have donated a single cent unless he actually had it—or a substantial limit on his credit card.

"I refuse to let you go into debt simply to prove a point," she snapped.

"First off, I won't go into debt. I have the money, and a fair amount more where that came from. Second, I'm not trying to prove a point. Unless I did." He winked at her. "In that case—"

"You're broke. You're always broke." It was another of the reasons Frankie hadn't told him about the girls. He couldn't afford the child support payments, and she hated the idea of a long, drawn-out court battle, only to have him default.

"I've had a run of good luck lately," he said.

"You rob a bank?"

"Come on. Give me a little credit. How 'bout

I tell you what's been happening with me over dinner tonight?"

Frankie's sisters were literally sitting on the edges of their seats.

"No." Dinner sounded too much like a date. "I'll bring some brisket and ribs to the park. The picnic area. You recall where it is?"

"I do."

Something flashed in his eyes. A memory, perhaps. He had plenty to choose from involving the park and the picnic area and the two of them. What had possessed Frankie to suggest that as a meeting place?

Mel abruptly straightened. "I'll watch the g—" She caught herself in the nick of time. "Feed the dogs. I'll feed your dogs if Sam can't."

"Sam?" Spence's eyes lit up. "The new sister? Mel and Ronnie mentioned that she's living with you. I'd love hearing about her at dinner." He was at it again, teasing her in order to get his way.

"We're not having dinner," she stated. "Consider the food a sample. If you're going to be an investor in my company, you should taste the wares."

Where had that come from? Frankie was clearly losing her mind.

She quickly jotted her down her phone number on a paper napkin and handed it to him.

"I can't wait." He scooted out of the booth.

She wasn't fast enough, and he brushed up beside her. The electric shock, even from such fleeting contact, was intense. Frankie sucked in a sharp breath.

Tugging on the brim of his cowboy hat, he ambled over to the counter where, thank goodness, the other waitress served him his breakfast order.

She didn't realize she was staring until Mel hitched a thumb at her. "Look at that, Ronnie. She's still hung up on him."

Frankie pivoted in time to see her younger sister nodding in agreement.

"For the record," she muttered, "you two couldn't be more wrong."

Hurrying off, she went to properly introduce herself to the new manager. It was that or deal with Spence. At the moment, Tia Maria's nephew seemed the lesser of two evils.

Chapter Two

"Feed the dogs?" Frankie rolled her eyes at Mel, who shrugged in reply.

"It was the best I could come up with spur of the moment."

The two of them were in Frankie's kitchen. Mel sat at the table while Frankie stood at the counter, packing the picnic dinner. Coleslaw? Seriously? Had she chosen that side dish simply because Spence liked her recipe?

She purposely included a small jar of bread-and-butter pickles in the cooler. *Her* favorite. Spence preferred kosher dills. She did, however, select the best pieces of barbecue beef. Only because she had a reputation to consider. And, were she honest with herself, an ego that knew no bounds when it came to her specialties.

"I'm sorry you didn't get the manager job." Mel tugged on the empty adjacent chair, bringing it closer and elevating her feet. "That's just not right."

"It's her restaurant. Tia Maria can hire whomever she wants as manager."

"But her nephew?" Mel snorted. "I heard he hasn't worked in the food industry since college and then as a waiter in a pizza joint."

News did travel fast in a small town. "He has a degree in business," Frankie said.

"Not the same."

"I didn't have any experience when Tia Maria hired me."

"You didn't start out as manager, either. You worked your way up. The hard way, I might add."

"There's no point rehashing this. She gave the

job to someone else. End of story. Seeing as I'm not prepared to quit, I'm staying."

Mel looked contrite. "And here I am pouring salt in the wound."

Frankie closed the lid on the remaining brisket and returned the storage container to the refrigerator. At the last second, she grabbed a triangle of leftover cherry pie. Adding that to the cooler, she checked the time.

"I'd better hurry."

At the thought of seeing Spence again, her stomach twisted into a knot and sweat broke out on her brow. This was a crazy idea. Maybe she should call and cancel.

No. She had to find out why he was here, how long he intended to stay and if he'd by chance become father material in these past four years. Only then could she tell him about Paige and Sienna.

From the living room, she heard the girls playing animal hospital with their stuffed toys, a game inspired by their veterinarian aunt. Giggling and lively chatter assured Frankie that her daughters were getting along for a change.

"I appreciate you watching Paige and Sienna."

"Are you kidding? I love babysitting. And it's good practice." Mel patted her protruding belly. "Besides, Aaron's on duty until ten tonight."

"You two set a date yet?"

Her cheeks colored. "Actually, we did."

"When?" Frankie hurried over to give her sister a hug.

"The Saturday before Thanksgiving."

"Why didn't you say something? That's only six weeks away. You can't possibly pull off a wedding by then."

"We're having a small ceremony," Mel assured her. "Family and close friends. Aaron already had the big shindig with his late wife. I wanted something different. Special and unique for us two."

"I'll cater the reception, of course." Frankie paused. "You are having one?"

"Yes." Mel laughed. "And I wouldn't dream of having a reception without your food."

"Let me know what else I can do to help."

Frankie was already contemplating contacting her sisters and stepmom about throwing a bridal shower. They'd better hurry. Next up would be a baby shower. Mel and Aaron may be planning a small wedding, but with the local vet marrying the local deputy, half the town would probably want an invite to one shower or the other.

A ping sounded from the table, Frankie's phone emitting another alert. She quickly snatched it and checked the screen. Not a donation notice from her crowd-funding campaign. Just a text from her other sister. She set the phone down.

"That's Ronnie. She says practice will run late again tonight, and Sam won't be home until ten or ten-thirty."

"She's really working hard."

Sam had turned professional barrel racer after graduating high school and had her heart set on winning a championship title. To accomplish that, she'd first need to qualify for the National

Finals Rodeo in December. With Ronnie's expert help, her chances were good.

"She's determined to come back after this last run of bad luck." Frankie tucked her phone into her purse, which was hanging from the back of a chair. "Two disqualifications in a row and a tenth place. She's frustrated."

"She's also young," Mel said. "If not this year, there's always next."

"Yeah. That's what Ronnie said for ten straight years. She qualified I forget how many times, but never won." It was their younger sister's biggest regret.

Frankie set the cooler on the table. All that remained was to get herself ready.

"There's leftover macaroni and cheese and fruit salad for the girls." She wagged a finger at Mel. "No soda or sweets. I don't care what *you're* craving."

It was Mel's turn to roll her eyes. "I got this. Quit worrying."

"I should be back long before their bedtime."

"Don't rush. You and Spence have a lot of catching up to do."

Frankie wished her sister would quit smiling. "I'm going to change."

In the bedroom, she took much too long choosing what shorts and top to wear. In the bathroom, she fussed with her hair and makeup.

What had Spence seen when he'd looked at her this morning? Frankie was no longer the thin young woman with long blond hair and an enviable complexion. Her figure had filled out a little after giving birth to her daughters, and she'd cut her hair, opting for a more trouble-free style. Her brown eyes were the same, but these days her skin's glow came from a bottle of foundation.

Refusing to admit how nervous she was, she dwelled instead on Spence's return. If she lived to be a hundred, she would never understand why her sisters had told him about her crowd-funding campaign. When Frankie demanded an explanation, Mel had said they were proud of her and wanted to brag. Besides, he'd asked

if she was still catering. What were they supposed to say?

A short while later Frankie returned to the
kitchen, as ready as she'd ever be. Mel pulled
her head out of the open refrigerator and gave
her a once-over.

"Nice."

"I just threw on the first thing I grabbed."
True. After ripping a half-dozen other outfits
from her closet, she'd ultimately settled on her
original selection.

"Still planning on telling him about..." Mel
tilted her head toward the living room, where
the girls were now wrapping their stuffed toys
with toilet paper bandages.

She sighed. "Not sure it'll be tonight. But, yes.
I just wish he was more reliable."

Mel came away from the refrigerator with fixings for the girls' dinner. "But he likes kids,
right?"

"He used to, anyway. I always thought he'd
make a good father. Except for not wanting to
settle down." Or get married. But that hadn't

stopped Frankie from falling in love. "Did he happen to say where he was working these days?"

"No, and we didn't ask."

Frankie was still grappling with his generous donation and claim to have plenty of money. Also, the fact that if she accepted his donation, she'd have to give him an ownership share of her company. Hopefully, he wouldn't bring up the subject tonight, but give her another day at least to get a better idea of why he was here, how long he was staying and what his future plans were, if any.

She mentally recounted all the jobs he'd had that she knew about. Rodeoing—until he tore his shoulder and had to quit. Ranch hand. Horse trainer. Trail guide for a wilderness outfitter. He'd even done a stint one season at a Wild West theme park, driving a stagecoach. She'd long ago lost track of how many different states he'd resided in.

Last she'd heard, over a year ago, through a friend of a friend of a friend, he was in California, working at a racing quarter horse farm. Frankie couldn't imagine what he was doing there. Handler? Groom? Certainly not a jockey. He had the horse skills, but at six foot two, he was far too big.

She doubted he'd changed his wandering ways. Why else would he have unexpectedly arrived in Mustang Valley, other than a quick pass through town on his latest adventure? He probably assumed she'd softened after all this time. Well, he was in for a surprise.

Before leaving, Frankie went into the living room, where she kissed the girls and extracted promises from them to be good for Auntie Mel. At the door, her sister patted her on the back as if she needed moral support, which, perhaps, she did.

"Call me if there's a problem." With a last goodbye, Frankie was gone.

During the short drive to the park in the center of town, she couldn't shake the feeling that the next few hours were going to have a huge impact on her life, if only because Spence might be learning he was a father.

How would he react? Run far and fast? Angrily accuse her of lying to him and go after her for custody of the girls? Insinuate himself into their lives?

He had made that donation to her crowd-funding campaign. According to the stated terms, donations of a thousand dollars or more entitled the contributor to a share in her company—until, and if, she bought them out. With interest, of course. Ten thousand dollars would entitle Spence to a...she didn't want to think about that.

Frankie arrived early. Typical. She was a bit obsessive-compulsive when it came to not making people wait, something she herself hated.

All six picnic tables were empty, though a few children played in the nearby playground under the supervision of their parents, and a young couple rode their horses along the designated equestrian trail. At dinnertime on a weekday evening, the park was bound to be empty.

By six, her and Spence's agreed-upon time, she had various covered containers unpacked and arranged. At five minutes past six, she huffed and checked her watch again.

Her anger returned, overpowering her nervousness. She should have expected this. He didn't know the meaning of punctual. Her glance constantly traveling to the parking area, she alternated between sitting, standing, pacing and gnashing her teeth.

Two vehicles arrived: one a compact car and the other a brand-new, fire-engine-red dually pickup with all the bells and whistles. She immediately dismissed the compact car as something Spence wouldn't drive. Could the truck be his? It did seem a bit much. She'd never seen him drive anything that wasn't destined for the junkyard.

Another ten minutes. That was the most she'd give him. If he didn't show by then, she was leaving. When a lone, tall man wearing a cowboy hat emerged from the pickup, Frankie's heart gave an abrupt leap. It *was* Spence. How in the world—

He came toward her, his stride easy and confident, his trademark sexy grin firmly in place. As he neared, he removed his sunglasses and slipped them into his front shirt pocket.

She'd worried earlier about how she looked to him. Older. Less attractive. A duller version of her younger self. What she should have worried about was how he looked to her. Good. As appealing as always. Lip-smacking gorgeous.

Frankie knew in that instant she hadn't changed one bit and was in serious danger of falling under his spell again. She struggled to shore up her defenses. Except she didn't have a chance before Spence reached her and swept her into a hug.

Not a rib-crushing, good-to-see-an-old-friend hug but the heady, twirl-in-a-circle, steal-your-breath-away kind.

What am I going to do now?

He set her down. Fortunately, he didn't let go

of her arm or she might have stumbled. He'd left her that disconcerted and that unsteady.

Pretending to have caught her sandal heel in a hole, she insisted, "I'm fine," and tried to extract her arm from his grasp.

He held firm, his glance roving her face before moving lower. "Yes, you are."

"Spence." She tugged harder. When was he ever not pouring on the charm?

"Sorry I'm late." He finally released her.

"What was it this time?" She couldn't keep the irritation from her voice. He always had one excuse or another. Flat tire. Dead battery. Traffic. A buddy who just happened to drop by.

"I had to make a few calls. The transport driver encountered flooding in Texas. He's going to be delayed a good half day."

"What's being transported?" She occupied herself with reorganizing the containers.

"I own two retired racing mares."

"Racing mares?"

He peered over her shoulder at the spread she'd prepared, getting a little too close for

Frankie's comfort. As if set on automatic, her body responded before she could stop herself, softening and leaning ever so slightly into him.

"We should probably sit down," he said, his breath tickling her neck. "A lot's happened these past few years."

Little did he know she could say the same thing.

IF IT WASN'T incredibly rude, Spence would have smacked his lips. "You could always cook, honey."

"Don't call me that. Please."

Frankie had quickly regained her composure and eased away from him. He liked knowing he could still rattle her. What he didn't like was the skittish look in her eyes. It was one thing for her to fight an attraction to him, another to be uneasy.

Popping the lids on various containers, she dealt paper plates as if they were cards from a deck. Next, she unwrapped the barbecue beef brisket he'd been dreaming about this entire past week, ever since deciding on returning to Mustang Valley.

All right, all right. Food wasn't all he'd been dreaming of. Luck had been on his side when he stopped by the café this morning and found Frankie's sisters there. He'd assumed she wouldn't be glad to see him, not after the last time he'd left and she told him in no uncertain terms to delete her number from his phone contacts.

And he'd been right. After her initial shock wore off, she'd fired an entire arsenal of invisible daggers at him.

Her sisters, however, had been happy to make room for him in the booth. They'd always liked him. And he'd liked the entire Hartman clan, which had apparently grown by a long-lost half sister and a brand-new stepmother.

With very little prodding, Mel and Ronnie had opened up, telling Spence the most important details—Frankie wasn't married and she wasn't currently seeing anyone.

Music to his ears. Though how some guy had

yet to put a ring on her finger baffled Spence. In his admittedly biased opinion, she was better looking now than ever. The short, chic hairstyle suited her, as did the stunning hourglass figure outlined by shorts and a snug top. Her brown eyes, when serious, had the power to captivate him, and make him laugh when twinkling with amusement.

She definitely wasn't amused now. Really? Just because he was a few minutes late?

"Would you like a beer?" she asked, her hand disappearing into the cooler.

He shook his head, reminding himself to focus. He likely had one chance with Frankie and didn't dare blow it.

"No, thanks. Lemonade's great."

"You're refusing a beer?" She turned to him, an incredulous expression on her face.

"I don't drink much anymore, except on special occasions."

"Since when?" She narrowed her gaze.

"No DUIs or mornings I regret or nights I

blacked out, if that's what you're thinking. I just cut back. Different lifestyle these days."

She handed him the lemonade she'd already poured, then grabbed another cup. "I forgot to ask earlier. Where are you staying?"

"Eddie's putting me up."

"Did he ever move out of that old double-wide trailer?"

"Are you kidding?" Spence took a swig of lemonade, sweetened exactly to his liking, then another. "At least I have my own room. With a bed." He'd spent many a night on a friend's couch or floor, more than he cared to admit. "But I have to figure out what to do with my mares. The transport truck will be here tomorrow afternoon."

"You shouldn't have much trouble. Plenty of places in the area accept temporary boarders."

Temporary? Was she fishing for information or insinuating he was leaving soon?

"Any suggestions?" he asked.

"Ronnie keeps her horses at Powell Ranch." She filled a plate with slices of brisket and

one big, meaty rib. Handing it to him, she indicated he should sit and help himself to the sides
and her homemade barbecue sauce. He noticed
right away she'd made coleslaw. His favorite.

"I'll check them out."

Spence had been casually acquainted with
the Powells at one time years ago. The family
owned the largest public horse stables in the
valley and had made a name for themselves
breeding and training mustangs—some of them
captured in the nearby McDowell Mountains.

"They have weekly rates," Frankie said. "For
short-term customers."

Definitely insinuating, Spence thought. He
should tell her of his plans, but decided to wait
and see how their dinner progressed.

Frankie sat down across from him. "So, tell
me about this different lifestyle of yours. And,
if I'm not being too nosy, how you came into
enough money that you can afford to invest ten
thousand dollars in a start-up business."

"The answer to both is the same."

He'd much rather she sat beside him. Not

going to happen, however. For a moment there, when he'd leaned close, he swore the old spark had flared between them. The next instant, she'd raised her guard.

On the drive here, Spence had worried that she'd agreed to meet with him only because of the money. Now, thanks to their mutual sparks, he knew that wasn't the case. She cared for him. A little, anyway. Even after their long separation.

He indulged in a bite of brisket, instantly forgetting where he was and what he was doing. "This is good. No, fantastic."

"It's better warm and freshly carved."

"Something to look forward to." Swallowing, he flashed her a grin. "Next time."

"You're changing the subject."

"Can't help myself, honey. I mean Frankie," he amended, before she could correct him. "This food is incredible. How is it you haven't opened up your own restaurant?"

"You were saying."

"Yes. Right. Different lifestyle." He fortified

himself with a heaping forkful of coleslaw. "Two years ago this spring, I took a job as assistant trainer for Cottonwood Farms. Have you heard of them?"

"Hmm. No." She concentrated on her plate, delicately picking at her food. "But someone did say you were working with racing quarter horses."

"Up until recently, Cottonwood Farms was a small player. Not anymore. The owner quite literally invested everything he had in a young colt named Han Dover Fist. The colt went on to be the top winning quarter horse last year, making his owners very rich."

"We don't hear much about horse racing of any kind in this part of the state."

Spence figured as much. Mustang Valley was a cattle ranching community, its horses primarily working stock or those ridden for pleasure. Probably only a few people realized one of the better known quarter horse racetracks was a mere hundred miles away, outside Tucson. Spence did, and while not the reason he'd returned, it certainly was an added benefit. He'd be making a trip there in the near future.

Picking up the Fred Flintstone–size rib Frankie had given him, he said, "I didn't think I'd like training racehorses. It's a lot different than cutting or calf roping. Turns out I'm pretty good."

"That where you're working now?" She dabbed at the corner of her mouth with a napkin. "Cottonwood Farms?"

Spence remembered what it was like to kiss those lovely, full lips, and the thrill that coursed through him when they parted beneath his. Clearing his throat and banishing distracting thoughts, he continued.

"I was up until a couple months ago."

"Ah."

He knitted his brows. "What does that mean?"

"Two years. That's a pretty long time to stick with one job. For you."

"It's not what you think."

"Enlighten me."

While she'd delivered the statement with a

teasing tone, there was no mistaking the seriousness of it. She saw him as a drifter. Unable or unwilling to hold down a job for very long.

"I guess you could say I'm on leave, with an invitation to return at any time."

"Why on leave?"

"I'm trying my hand at racehorse breeding. Which is why I purchased the two retired mares. They were sold at a good price. One I couldn't turn down."

"Even at a good price, they couldn't have been cheap." She propped her elbows on the table. "Do you mind me asking where you got the money?"

"Well, that's where the story gets interesting."

"I bet."

"Betting does have something to do with it, yes." He pushed aside his plate. Not because he was full, but because he wanted to watch the play of emotions on Frankie's face. "Buying Han Dover Fist drained my boss's finances. He didn't have enough money to pay me full wages, so we worked out an agreement. I helped train the colt in exchange for an ownership share."

"You might have wound up working for nothing."

"But I didn't. Han Dover exceeded everyone's expectations. He was the long shot in more than one race at the beginning of last year. I would scrape together what cash I could and bet on him to win."

Interest flared in her eyes. "Is that where you got the ten thousand dollars? Gambling winnings?"

"No. My gambling winnings are what I used to buy the mares." At fifty-to-one odds that first race, Spence had done okay for himself. He'd quadrupled those winnings over the next three months.

"You must have believed in the horse."

"I did. And not just because I helped train him. At the end of the season, my boss paid me a bonus on top of my share of the winnings. There are also stud fees, which will roll in for as long as I own a percentage of Han Dover Fist."

She blinked in disbelief. "Are you making this up?"

"Every word I've said is true. I'm not rich, but I have a nice nest egg in the bank, and if all goes well, I'll have my own racing quarter horse farm."

"That's a pretty ambitious dream."

Spence took her hand, half expecting her to snatch it away. She didn't.

"I know what you're thinking. I've moved from job to job, place to place, and rarely had two nickels to rub together. But the fact is, I've changed."

"So you say."

He was a bit wounded by her disbelief in him. "I've worked hard and have something to show for it. I also intend to keep working hard and have more to show."

"Horse racing—" she reclaimed her hand in order to shoo away a pesky fly "—is a risky business. It's also a rich man's business."

She wasn't wrong. Plenty of people went broke. A few lucky ones, like his boss, made a fortune. If they had the right horse. Spence had high hopes for the foals his pregnant mares were carrying.

"I'm smart," he said. "I'm starting small and not investing any more money than I can afford to lose."

She glanced away, staring unseeingly at the play area.

"I've disappointed you in the past," he said gently. "Plenty. I get why you think I'm chasing rainbows. But aren't you doing the same thing with your catering business?"

Her head snapped back around. "It's a lot less risky. And besides, I have a steady day job. One that provides benefits."

"True. But if I lost everything I have now, I wouldn't be worse off than when I started. Better, in fact. I have a job waiting for me."

She frowned. "That's not a very responsible attitude. Lose everything?"

"Believe me—I intend to be a success."

She looked away again.

"I get it. My track record doesn't inspire confidence." He paused and started over. "I really believe I bounced around so much because I was searching for this. I love what I'm doing, Frankie."

"Is it the excitement?" she asked.

"I won't deny horse racing is fun. Nothing compares to the thrill of watching a horse you helped train cross the finish line in first place."

"Nothing?"

Was she referring to herself or what they once had together?

"Nothing work-related." He tried again to express himself. "I'm good at this, Frankie. Just like you're good at cooking. And I'm convinced I can make a decent living. Also like you. We aren't that different."

"Why did you come back?" She not only returned her attention to him, she stared intently.

"To see you. Now that I finally have something to offer. I'm hoping you'll…reconsider. Give me another chance."

"You hurt me, Spence. A lot. You know I wanted to get married eventually and have a family. Yet you left. Again. I got the message loud and clear. You weren't ready."

He blew out a long, resigned breath. "I can't tell you how many regrets I have."

"I'm not sure I can trust you."

"I've changed. I swear." Even as the words left his mouth, he realized he'd said them before. "This time, it's true."

She hesitated. Well, at least she wasn't telling him to get the hell out of Mustang Valley and never come back.

"I need time," she finally said. "To think."

"Sure. Sure."

"I'm not the same person, either. A lot's different."

"I want to hear all about it."

"Give me until tomorrow." Though they weren't quite done eating, she began putting food away. "Meet me at the café. Ten thirty sharp. We can talk before my shift starts at noon."

"Okay."

"Don't be late," she added.

He chuckled. "What? Is this a test?"

"As a matter of fact, it is." She abruptly stood and sent him a look that left no doubt.

Chapter Three

Frankie sat at a booth in the café, waiting for Spence and staring at her phone. Swiping her finger across the screen, she read and reread the terms of her equity crowd-funding campaign. What had struck her as simple and straightforward when she started her campaign now appeared confusing.

Never in her wildest dreams had she imagined someone donating a thousand dollars, much less ten thousand. If she upheld the terms of her campaign, and accepted Spence's money, he'd own 10 percent of her company. A company that, without him, was no more than a glorified hobby.

The thought staggered her. And scared her.

On the one hand, Spence offered her the chance to realize her long-held hope of owning her own business. On the other hand, the offer came with strings. Lots of them.

Groaning softly, she set her phone down, angry at herself for stalling. The big issue wasn't her crowd-funding, it was telling—or not telling—Spence about their daughters, Paige and Sienna.

"You want a refill?"

Frankie glanced up to find her coworker brandishing a pot of coffee.

"I'm good. Thanks."

She was already unnerved at the prospect of seeing Spence for the second time in less than twenty-four hours. More coffee would literally give her the shakes.

"I was going to ask you," the young woman said, leaning closer. "Would it be all right if I took tomorrow off? I know it's late notice, but Shelly Anne said she would swap days with me."

Frankie shrugged. "I'm okay with it, but you'd better talk to Antonio. He has the final say." She barely hid her frustration.

"Yeah. Hmm." The young woman frowned. "What do you make of him?"

"He seems nice enough. I only spent about an hour with him. We're supposed to work together on the inventory this afternoon."

"He has no experience. You should have gotten the job," the woman added in a hushed voice.

Frankie glanced at the pass-through window, where the top halves of Cook and Antonio could be seen, the two of them moving back and forth in front of the grill. Tia Maria had decided her nephew should train with Cook today, learning the ins and outs of how the kitchen functioned.

"It is what it is," Frankie said. "But I appreciate the support."

"What are you going to do?"

She thought again of Spence, her crowd-funding campaign and breaking the news to him that he was a father. "I'm not sure. Maybe nothing. Maybe surprise everyone."

A customer two booths over hailed the waitress. She lightly touched Frankie's shoulder before murmuring, "See you later," and hurrying away.

Frankie closed the open web page on her phone, simultaneously checking the time. Ten fifteen. She'd warned Spence not to be late. Would he take her seriously or, as usual, come dragging in when he felt like it?

She swore she could feel the stares of half the café's customers boring into her. They'd probably heard Spence was back in town. Also that Tia Maria had hired her nephew. The customers no doubt wondered what she was doing here, sitting in a booth rather than waiting on them. Who came to their place of employment during their time off?

Someone preferring neutral territory to converse with the man who'd shaped her entire past and could conceivably alter her entire future.

"Hey, there, Frankie."

Another interruption. This time from one of her sister Mel's veterinarian clients.

"Hi. How you doing?"

"I could ask you the same thing." The trim and athletic senior woman didn't wait for an invitation and slipped into the booth across from Frankie. "I saw Spence this morning. He was at Powell Ranch. Did you know he's back in town?"

"Yes." She refused to say more.

"I overheard him chatting with the Powells about boarding a couple of horses."

"Really?" Frankie didn't let on he'd already told her this.

"He must be staying in town, then."

"I…couldn't say."

Disappointment shone on the woman's face. She'd obviously been hoping for more of a reaction from Frankie.

Unbelievably, the subject of their conversation breezed into the café, the glass door whooshing closed behind him.

"Great," Frankie muttered under her breath.

The one time Spence arrived promptly, and she had to be sitting with someone itching for a repeat-worthy moment. "I, um, hate to ask you to…"

What should she say? Please leave?

Of course, Spence spotted her immediately and came right over, returning the greetings given him from various old friends, but not stopping.

Frankie had barely caught her breath when he appeared at the table, grinning broadly, looking scrumptious and not at all fazed to find someone with her.

"Morning," he addressed the woman. "We run into each other again."

"Yes, we do." Her glance traveled between him and Frankie. "I didn't realize you were waiting for him."

Frankie's hands betrayed her, starting to tremble. She hid them beneath the table, cursing the coffee she'd drunk and knowing it wasn't the cause.

"Am I late?" he asked.

"No. I just got here." Did half an hour ago count as "just"?

"You ready?" He held out his hand.

What the heck was going on?

"If you don't mind." He turned his attention to the other woman, who stared at him with wide eyes. "Frankie and I don't have much time."

Frankie grimaced. As if tongues weren't already wagging.

"Don't let me hold you up." The woman vacated the booth.

Frankie suddenly realized Spence was rescuing her from an uncomfortable situation. Not causing trouble. When had he become astute enough to read other people's feelings, and thoughtful enough to respond?

"Uh, yes." She tentatively accepted his hand and let him assist her from the booth. They started walking toward the door. "You can let go of me," she whispered.

"Come on. Let's really give them something to talk about."

It wasn't the stares bothering her. Not even

close. What worried Frankie was that the instant she and Spence had touched, familiar sensations stirred inside her. And rather than resist, she'd savored them.

Outside, she reclaimed her hand. "Where are we going?" Her original intention had been to talk in the café.

"Let's walk. I haven't had a chance to check out the town since I got back."

This time of year, mornings were cool enough to be outdoors. Within a few hours, however, the temperature would soar to the mideighties.

"As you can see," Frankie said, "things are mostly the same." At least walking provided an outlet for her nervous energy.

"I see the feed store has changed hands."

"The owner sold the store after his assistant manager was involved in a series of horse thefts around the valley."

"And your sister Mel helped catch the thieves. She's marrying the deputy who headed up their capture, right?"

"She tell you that yesterday?"

"Actually, I heard about it last month when I was passing through town."

"Why didn't you contact me?"

"The timing wasn't right."

Was it because he finally had money? Frankie had never cared that Spence wasn't wealthy. She'd grown up in a modest home, but one filled with love. Though she'd lost her mother at a young age, her father had done his best to ensure his daughters' happiness. She knew there were more important things in life than having a fat bank account.

They crossed the street at the corner and headed down the next block.

"What did you want to talk about?" he asked. "And for the record, I wasn't late."

No, he'd been early. "My catering business. I'm not sure you know, but a ten thousand dollar contribution entitles you to a 10 percent ownership and a share of the profits."

"Sounds a little like my arrangement with Han Dover Fist. I own 15 percent of him and get a share of the profits."

"Do you have a say in his management?" Frankie was genuinely curious.

"Not anymore. He's retired from the track and living the life of a king at Cottonwood Farms. Quit a winner—that was my boss's philosophy." Spence indicated a group of boisterous riders tying their horses to a hitching rail beside the Poco Dinero Bar and Grill. "I see that practice hasn't changed."

"And likely never will as long as we're a ranching community."

At the next corner, Spence asked, "What are your plans for the catering business? Mel and Ronnie mentioned you're just doing side jobs right now."

It was a reasonable question, especially from a potential investor. Besides, Frankie would rather talk about her business than the girls.

"I'd like to buy a smoker. Commercial grade, I should say. All I have now are two small ones. More chafing dishes. And warming boxes to transport food. Then there's advertising and promotion."

For the next five minutes, she outlined her ideas. Spence made several intelligent comments that had her contemplating her answers.

"Sounds good," he remarked when she was done.

"How involved would you expect to be?"

"Are you asking if I intend to stick around?" He flashed her the same happy grin he'd used back when they were dating, to lighten her mood or ease her worries.

"Honestly? Yes." She kept her voice level.

His response was more important to her than she cared to admit.

"I suppose it depends a lot on you."

"Me?" She stopped to look at him.

They stood in front of the auto parts store, with its slight smell of oil and flashing neon sign, lit even during the day. Not the most romantic setting.

"I'd like to stick around, Frankie. Mustang Valley is a good place for me to start my racing quarter horse farm."

"You said yesterday you wanted another chance with me."

"There's that, too."

They began walking again. "Not that it's any of my business," she said, finally giving in to her curiosity, "but have you met anyone these past four years?"

"I've dated a couple gals. Nothing serious." He chuckled, with more nervousness than humor. "I had a lot of trouble getting over you, Francine Hartman."

Then why didn't you come back? Her life, and that of her daughters, might now be entirely different.

"Let me rephrase," he said. "No one's compared to you."

"I see." She shouldn't be happy. And she wasn't.

Fine, fine. She was a little happy. She'd pined over him, too.

"What about you?" he asked. "Anybody special?"

"I know for a fact my sisters told you I'm single." *Damn them*, she thought.

Spence smiled sheepishly. "I just wanted to hear it from you."

She resisted. For two seconds. "I've dated, too. Nothing serious," she added, echoing him.

"Why not? You're a catch."

Frankie hesitated. She couldn't tell him she'd been too busy working and raising their daughters to give much thought to dating. Or that most single men weren't interested in a ready-made family.

"Lately, I've been busy trying to get my catering business off the ground."

"Nice pat answer. What's the real reason?"

Okay. He asked for it. "It's been hard for me to trust anyone again after you."

"Would it make a difference if I told you I wasn't the guy for you at the time, and that I was trying for a clean break? Much as I loved you, and I did, I couldn't bring myself to settle down and have that family you wanted."

"And now you're different?"

"Yes, I am." His confidence returned. "You *can* trust me."

She wasn't entirely swayed. But he had gone out on a limb to admit the truth to her, and that took courage.

"I have a short shift at the café. Come by my house tonight. Seven thirty."

His eyes sparked. "To talk business?"

"No."

"Now I'm intrigued."

She felt suddenly uncomfortable. "We'd better get back. My shift starts soon."

At the entrance to the café, he took her hand again. Only rather than hold it, he brought her palm to his cheek. The bristles of his day-old beard tickled her skin. "I meant what I said about staying. Give me a reason, Frankie, and I'm here for good."

She could do that, give him a reason. And throw him for a heck of a loop in the process.

"We'll talk more tonight." Her hand fell away from his face. "Goodbye, Spence." Hurrying inside, she quickly changed into her uniform, her fumbling fingers struggling with the zipper.

She didn't have much time. For all she knew, Eddie or someone else had already mentioned her girls, and Spence was biding his time, waiting for her to confess or to call her out on her unforgivable lie.

Just breathe. In and out.

Frankie stopped in the doorway and fought to slow her racing heart. The moment she'd been dreading for years had at long last arrived. No amount of panicking would delay it.

It HAD TAKEN every ounce of Spence's willpower not to follow Frankie inside the café earlier. He'd told her he wanted to stay in Mustang Valley, which in his mind amounted to admitting he still cared. Her response had been to stare blankly at him, and then suggest they get back.

Okay, he was man enough to admit that stung. Then again, she hadn't given him the boot. And she'd invited him to her house. He'd been contemplating the endless possibilities for hours.

Contrary to what he'd implied, his buddy Eddie had divulged very little about Frankie. Not that Spence had asked. He hadn't wanted to appear interested, which, of course, he was.

The house he pulled up in front of was in the new residential section of Mustang Valley, built less than a mile from the park and center of town. With its stucco siding and Santa Fe styling, he thought the home exactly the type Frankie would have picked. Someday, when she finally had that family she wanted. But now?

While far from huge, it did seem a lot for one person, especially with its spacious backyard and modest horse setup. That part struck Spence as odd, seeing as Frankie wasn't much into horses and livestock like the rest of her family, other than as a spectator. But, then again, most people in Mustang Valley owned horses, and most houses came with a horse setup.

Solar lights lined the walkway to Frankie's front door, casting slanted ovals of gold on the desert landscaping and reminding Spence of the late hour. Seven thirty? He pondered the reasoning behind Frankie's request as he knocked on her front door.

His pulse beat faster, revealing his anxiety. She answered quickly, making him think she'd been watching out the window. As the door swung open, he took in the sight of her, and his throat promptly went dry.

"You look great." So much for playing it cool. "Seriously, Frankie."

She gave him a once-over but, unlike him, managed to refrain from blurting the first thing to pop into her head.

"Come on in."

He stepped over the threshold and was instantly assaulted by a pair of friendly dogs, one a Lab mix and the other a yappy terrier. Both sniffed his pant legs and boots. Apparently, he passed inspection, for they quickly moved away, tails wagging and tongues lolling.

"I see you're still collecting strays." Spence

bent and gave each dog an ear scratching. "Where are the cats?"

"Cat," Frankie clarified. "And she's around somewhere."

She had a tender heart and was always rescuing one needy animal or another. Also, apparently, long-lost half sisters.

On quick inspection, he saw the living room was decorated with a few items he remembered from her dad's house. The oil painting hanging over the couch. The pine side table her grandfather had made. A braided rug beneath the table. Various pictures of little girls hung in a pattern on the wall. She and her sisters as children, Spence guessed.

"You have a nice place."

"We—I like it."

He followed her inside, quite enjoying the view. She paused and turned. He enjoyed this view even better.

Capri pants emphasized her shapely calves. Bare feet exposed red toenails. A gold chain circled her slim neck, the engraved disk nestled in her generous cleavage. A second gold chain circled her right ankle. Tiny crinkles that appeared at the corners of her eyes when she smiled had him falling for her all over again.

"Frankie." Unable to help himself, he reached for her. "I've missed you."

"Spence—"

He didn't give her time to finish and pulled her against him, aligning the body parts that mattered the most. "I've been waiting for this since I saw you in that ugly uniform yesterday." He dipped his head.

"Ugly—?"

He cut her off again, this time with a kiss. Her spine stiffened, and she resisted him. For a moment. And while not exactly surrendering, she did relax and let his mouth move over hers in a familiar pattern he'd dreamed about for four straight years.

Fire instantly flared inside him, the one only she could ignite. His hold on her tightened as he wrapped an arm around her waist and increased the pressure of his mouth, urging her lips to part. When they did, and he tasted her, the fire raged until it nearly consumed him.

The next instant, it died when she extracted herself from his embrace. "Not now," she said in a low voice, and stepped away, establishing a safe distance between them.

"All right."

Had he really just answered her with complete composure? She'd left him shaken, both because of the intensity of their kiss—incredibly potent even after all this time—and her unnerving calm. How could her world not be spinning? His was, wildly out of control.

Then again, she'd said, "Not now." She hadn't said, "Not ever again." Spence wasn't one to split hairs, but in his mind, there was a big difference.

"Have a seat." She gestured toward the couch.

"Thanks." He thought he detected a slight shakiness in her raised arm. Maybe she wasn't immune to him, after all.

Removing his cowboy hat, he placed it on the coffee table next to a stack of colorful books.

Dr. Seuss? Really? Must be more childhood mementoes. Taking a cue from the dogs, who'd already claimed nearby spots on the floor, he lowered himself onto the couch.

Was that a noise he heard from down the hall? Had Frankie left a TV on in the bedroom? Perhaps her sister Sam was here and had been issued strict instructions to stay out of sight while Spence was visiting.

"You've done well for yourself," he said.

"This is mostly Dad's doing. He won the lottery last spring. Maybe you heard."

"Your sisters mentioned something. I remember him buying tickets every week."

"Same numbers for over thirty years."

She chose the chair next to the side table rather than the end of the couch near him. Drat. Foiled again.

"It wasn't a fortune," she said. "But enough to make all our lives easier. Dad split the money four ways between himself, Mel, Ronnie and me. I used my share for a down payment on this house and some furnishings. He and Dolores were getting married, and I didn't want to be living with them."

"That was generous of him."

"It was. Ronnie started her barrel racing school with her share and Mel bought her vet practice. Dad paid for his wedding to Dolores and their honeymoon in Hawaii."

"You like her? Your stepmom?" Spence remembered the Frankie from high school who desperately missed her late mother and believed it was her job to help raise her younger sisters.

"She's wonderful. We love her to pieces."

"I'm surprised you didn't use your share to start your catering business."

"I thought about it. But getting my own place was more important. We were living wi—" She stopped herself, not for the first time tonight. "No new bride needs a third wheel."

"I suppose not."

A lull fell, one that Spence felt acutely. This wasn't typical. For them, conversation had always flowed easily.

"It's a good-size house," he said. "Lots of room for you and Sam. She lives with you, right?"

"She does, though she's with friends tonight." Frankie shifted uncomfortably. "Look, Spence. There's a reason I asked you over tonight and it has nothing to do with my catering business or us."

"Okay." His insides clenched, responding to the somber tone in her voice and worried expression on her face.

"Wait here." She rose. "Don't move. Promise me. I have two very special people I'd like you to meet."

She disappeared from the room and padded down the hall. Spence strained his ears, hearing voices. So he hadn't been wrong about someone else in the house. But who? Not a guy; she wasn't dating, and not Sam. Her stepmom maybe?

Finally, after what felt like an agonizing amount of time, Frankie reappeared, trailed by two little girls. What the heck…?

Stopping in the middle of the room, she gathered the girls to her sides. They were a study in contrast: one short and blonde, the other taller and with dark hair. Nonetheless, something made Spence think they were sisters.

"This is Paige—" Frankie lifted the shorter one's hand, clasped firmly in hers "—and this is Sienna." She patted the top of the taller one's head with her other hand. "My daughters."

Spence was never at a loss for what to say. Until now. He stared at Frankie and the girls, a malfunction occurring in the area of his brain responsible for speech.

Daughters? Impossible!

Well, apparently not, for there they stood, wearing matching pajamas and staring at him with a mixture of shyness and curiosity.

"Um…uh, hello," he managed to choke out.

"I thought you three should meet. Girls, say hi."

"Hi," they both said simultaneously and softly, clinging to their mother.

Their mother! Frankie had children. Two of

them! This explained the pictures on the wall and the Dr. Seuss books.

When had it happened? Well, obviously during the last four years. How old were they? Spence wasn't good at these things, having no experience. He was the youngest of three siblings and not a father himself. His oldest brother had children, but he and his wife lived in Marana. Spence visited them only once or twice a year.

"We're twins," the shorter one said, as if she made that announcement regularly.

"Really? You don't look alike."

"They're fraternal twins," Frankie explained.

Whatever that meant. Not wishing to appear stupid, Spence said nothing.

"I'm older." Again, the smaller one spoke. "Six minutes."

"Then how come you're smaller?"

"Grandpa says I'm still growing."

Did the taller one talk at all? Spence looked at her closely. Large, expressive eyes. Brown hair straight and thick as a horse's tail. She reminded him of someone, though he couldn't put his finger on who. The shorter one was the spitting image of Frankie. A Hartman through and through.

"Well," she started, "I just wanted to introduce you before I put them to bed. Say goodnight, girls."

They did, and Frankie escorted them back to their bedroom.

Unable to just sit there after they left, Spence sprang up from the couch and crept along the entryway leading down the hall. There, he waited and listened to Frankie conversing with her daughters as she tucked them in bed.

She was sweet with them, making promises for the next day, reciting a good-night prayer and telling them to "Sleep tight." He was admittedly touched.

Before she turned off the light, Spence crept away and resumed his seat on the living room couch. His entire body shook, the result of shock and wonder and surprise. He'd returned to Mustang Valley thinking, hoping, possibly to win Frankie back.

Her having daughters changed that. Spence wasn't sure he was ready to step into the role of parent, even a stepparent.

His first instinct was to leave town. But then, wasn't that always his first plan of action? And probably what Frankie expected of him. She could be testing him again, like she had this morning about being on time. He'd bragged to her he was a changed man. Leaving town would show he'd lied.

But daughters. Two of them. He was entitled to be taken aback. And reevaluating his return to Mustang Valley in order to woo Frankie was completely understandable.

Hearing her sigh, he glanced up.

She smiled weakly. "That took longer than I thought. Didn't mean to keep you waiting."

"No worries." He stood and reached for his cowboy hat. The idea of stealing a good-night kiss had also vanished. "It's getting late. And you're busy. I should probably go."

He saw the look in her eyes, silently accusing him of running. Damn. He just couldn't stop himself and turned toward the door.

"Wait, Spence." She hadn't moved. "There's something else I need to tell you."

There was more? He tried to grin, certain it fell flat. "Sure. What?"

"Paige and Sienna. Aren't you the least bit curious about their father?"

"I figured you'd tell me if you wanted me to know."

She gazed directly at him, and her stare was so powerful and unwavering, Spence tensed. His gut screamed she was about to deliver life-altering news.

"I should have told you sooner." She inhaled, then blew out slowly. "And I certainly understand if you're angry at me."

"Why would I be angry?"

Suddenly, everything clicked into place, and he knew her answer before she spoke.

"You're their father, Spence. Paige and Sienna are your daughters."

Chapter Four

Spence's vision dimmed to a hazy gray. He was aware of his surroundings and the words Frankie had spoken—*Paige and Sienna are your daughters*—but nothing made sense.

Sweat broke out on his forehead. He swore he could feel each and every bead forming. Hearing a muffled thump, he looked down at his cowboy hat on the floor. Glaring at his hands as if they were at fault, he bent and retrieved the hat. The motion caused a dizzying sensation, as if he were on an elevator that had stopped too fast.

He was a father? Impossible! Frankie would have told him. If not her, someone else. He'd been back in Mustang Valley for two days. Passed through last month. Surely a "Visiting your daughters?" or "Wondered when you were going to do right by those youngsters," would have slipped out.

Unless someone *had* said something. There was that remark the ranch hand at Powell Ranch made about seeing his girls. Spence had assumed he misunderstood and the guy said girl singular, meaning Frankie. He'd responded with a grin and "Heading to the café shortly." Then there was the woman behind the counter at the market. She'd said, "Guess Frankie finally convinced you to come back," with a knowing grin. Now, Spence understood what had been behind that grin.

He whirled on Frankie, his anger erupting. "You lied to me."

"Yes." She didn't have the decency to look him in the face.

"For years. I had a right to know."

"I'm sorry, Spence." Finally, she raised her gaze to his. Tears filled her eyes.

"That's all you have to say? I'm sorry?"

Her glance cut to the hallway. "Please. Not so loud."

"They don't know I'm their father?"

She shook her head.

"What did you tell them? Have they even asked about me?"

"Of course they've asked." She swallowed. "I said he was a man I'd been in love with since I was fifteen. But that he had to leave before they were born because he has a job in California."

"That's it?"

"Well, a little more," she admitted. "But I keep my explanations simple. Only answer the questions they ask. I did say you were coming back one day."

"Great. Now they think I abandoned them. I never took you for being cruel, Frankie."

His remark obviously cut deep, for more tears filled her eyes. But she had been cruel, by not telling him he was a father and then lying to the girls about why he wasn't a part of their lives.

"They're three, Spence. I'm not sure they're mature enough to think you abandoned them."

"You made me out to be the bad guy when you're the one who lied. To me and to them. But, hey, they're probably not mature enough to realize that."

She straightened her spine. "I did what I thought was best at the time."

"For who? You?"

She and Spence stood in the middle of the living room, facing each other, when he wasn't turning and pacing in frustration.

"Yes, for me," she admitted softly.

"How? Why was it best for you?"

"Lots of reasons. You were unreliable. Gone for months at a time, jumping from job to job. You didn't want kids. You said so yourself, more than once. You weren't ready to settle down. What was I supposed to do? Say, 'Surprise, you're a dad'?"

"Those are just excuses to justify your actions."

She sniffed, visibly composing herself. "Well, we can't change what happened. We can only move forward."

"You were on birth control. We were careful."

"It failed."

A memory suddenly resurfaced. "Is that why you insisted I never come back that last time? Because you were pregnant?"

"No. I swear I didn't discover I was pregnant until three weeks after you left. I insisted you never come back because I was mad at you and hurt."

"And still mad when the doctor gave you the test results?"

"I was confused."

Spence groaned and shoved his fingers through his hair, feeling the damp strands against his skin. "And when exactly did you become unconfused? Oh, wait. You haven't. Because we both know if not for me showing up yesterday, you and I wouldn't be having this conversation."

Her answer was to blush a vivid pink. Or was that an angry pink? "You have to admit you weren't ready to embrace fatherhood."

His anger reached a whole new level. "Me not being ready to embrace fatherhood isn't the problem here. It's you and the giant lies you've told."

"I had a high-risk pregnancy. Comes with having twins." Her chin trembled slightly. "The doctor insisted I avoid as much stress as possible. Every time I thought of telling you, I'd panic."

"Wow." Spence chuckled drily. "Now you're blaming the pregnancy."

"It's true. I did have a difficult time."

"Did it ever occur to you I might have made that time easier for you, not harder?"

She breathed deeply. "Mostly, I was scared."

At last! They were getting closer to the truth. "Did you think I wouldn't step up?"

"No. I was sure you would."

"Then why?" Spence moved closer, wanting, needing to know the answer.

"I was afraid you'd insist we get married." Her voice grew small. "And that I'd say yes. We'd have both wound up miserable. You, because you were forced into a life you didn't want. Me, because I was the one responsible for forcing you. Mostly, I was afraid you'd grow to hate me."

Spence considered what she'd said, and his anger slowly abated. He would have asked her to marry him. And, in those days, he might have grown to resent her for tying him down with a wife and children.

Then. Now, he was a different person. And though having children wasn't in his immediate plans, he had begun to see them as a possibility a few years down the road. Once his horse farm was more established. Spence did have his priorities and was determined to spend his money wisely.

Wait a minute...

"Is that why you told me now? Because I have money when I didn't before?"

Frankie recoiled in shock. "Absolutely not!"

"You could sue me for back child support."

Could she? He'd better find out.

"I doubt it, since I didn't tell you about the girls."

"Are you sure about that?"

She paused. "I don't know. I won't sue, however."

"Come on, Frankie. What other reason was there for telling me?"

She crossed her arms defiantly. "If I was after your money, you'd have heard from my attorney by now."

"Maybe you'll hear from mine."

"You do what you need to, Spence."

She was getting testy, which annoyed him. He'd done nothing wrong. Even if he'd made a few unkind remarks, his reaction was expected. She'd dropped a hell of a bombshell and done him a terrible injustice.

"Why now?" he repeated. "Is me coming back the reason?"

"Yes. I figured sooner or later you'd hear, and I wanted to be the one to tell you."

Her honesty surprised him even as it disappointed him. He'd hoped she felt compelled to tell him because it was the right thing to do. Apparently not.

"I heard a couple remarks. I just didn't put two and two together. I was too focused on you and picking up where we left off."

"Oh."

Her clipped response told him she considered that objective off the table. Well, maybe it was.

"Say I hadn't come back. Were you ever going to say something? Seriously?"

"Yes. Absolutely. I've been thinking about it a lot recently." Her demeanor changed. Softened. "Did my sisters mention how we met Sam?"

"She showed up a couple months ago at your dad's birthday party. Until then, none of you knew she existed."

"Dad had a relationship with a woman after

Mom died and never told us. In his defense, we were young and hadn't gotten over losing Mom. He waived his parental rights, and Sam's stepdad adopted her when she was a baby. It wasn't until she was sixteen that she learned the truth."

Spence found himself relating to Sam. She, too, had been lied to, in this case about her father. "Poor kid. That must have been hard on her."

"Which is why I opened my home and my heart to her. But it also got me thinking. Sam missed out on having a relationship with her biological father for almost her entire life. I didn't want the same thing to happen to Paige and Sienna."

"What about my parents. Did it occur to you they've been denied knowing their grandchildren?"

"Yes." Frankie's shoulders sagged, and she looked suddenly tired.

"They're going to be hurt when they find out. Which might have been years from now."

"I'm not certain when I would have told you. But soon," Frankie insisted.

He wasn't convinced. Nonetheless, he let her remark slide. "I don't want to fight."

"Me either."

"I need some time to sort through…everything." He rubbed his temples. His head didn't exactly hurt. More like it felt stretched to its limit, having been overfilled with information.

"I understand."

"Just so you know, things will be different. I'm going to be a part of Paige and Sienna's lives."

It was, he realized, the first time he'd spoken their names.

"I'm glad to hear that."

She didn't sound glad. Pretty much the opposite.

He shoved his cowboy hat down onto his head. "I'll call you tomorrow. When's a good time?"

"I'm off work. The girls' preschool is closed for Columbus Day. We'd planned on staying home."

"How's ten?"

"Fine."

Spence had his own list of tasks to accomplish. In between, he'd contemplate his next step and make some calls. His boss at Cottonwood Farms was smarter than most and had dealt with his share of family problems. He might prove to be a good sounding board.

Before turning toward the door, Spence paused. "I want to tell the girls I'm their father. As soon as possible."

Panic bloomed on Frankie's face. "I'd like to wait a little while."

"Why? To see if I'm going to stick around?"

"To prepare them first. I'm not being unreasonable."

"Neither am I."

"I refuse to let you break their hearts, Spence. They're innocent and don't deserve to be hurt and disappointed."

Like you hurt and disappointed me. He could hear what she'd left unspoken.

"You owe me, Frankie."

She stiffened. "I'm just asking."

"Me, too."

"We'll talk more tomorrow."

He'd been dismissed. Much like four years ago, when he'd told her he was hitting the road again for a wrangler job in Colorado. He ground his teeth together.

"Mommy?"

They both spun to see the taller girl—Sienna?— standing in the doorway.

"What's wrong, sweetie?" Frankie rushed over to her.

"I can't sleep."

"Let's get you back to bed." She peered over her shoulder at Spence. "Can you see yourself out?"

Definitely being dismissed. He walked out the door, closing it behind him. In the truck, he fumbled with the keys, which didn't seem to fit into the ignition.

Rather than go straight to Eddie's double-wide, Spence stopped at the local market for a six-pack of beer. This was a special occasion; he'd just learned he was a father. Of twins. That certainly entitled him to a beer. Eddie would definitely join him.

Dropping the six-pack on the counter, he reached into his back pocket for his wallet.

"Stocking up for the road?" the clerk asked. She was the same one who'd made a remark yesterday Spence had misconstrued.

"I don't drink and drive," he said in a steely voice, and handed over enough money to cover the beer.

She appeared not to notice his annoyance. "Thought you might be leaving town again."

Like he had before? Was Spence that predictable?

Reality sank in, with the force of an anvil falling from a third-story window. He was a father! Of twin girls. He had a responsibility and a duty. To them and Frankie.

"I'm not going anywhere." He grabbed the beer and his change. "Not this time."

FRANKIE DIDN'T LIKE relying on television to babysit Paige and Sienna. This was one of those times, however, when breaking her own rule was the lesser of two evils. Her mind was too overworked with thoughts of Spence and last night, her body too tired from lack of sleep, for her to be the ideal mother.

What had he done when he left? How was he feeling this morning? He'd been so angry with her. And confused. Well, who wouldn't be?

Had the morning brought any clarity to him? Waiting to hear was hard, but Frankie didn't think she had much choice. Better she wait for him to make the next move.

She checked the kitchen clock. It read ten twenty. Hadn't he said he'd call at ten? She supposed he could be busy.

Unless he'd chosen to leave town. He had before.

The girls clearly didn't mind watching TV. They sat on the family room floor, alternately giggling and squabbling, whispering and tumbling, tickling and teasing each other while a Disney movie played on the TV. The dogs lay nearby, snoozing and completely disinterested even when Paige galloped her stuffed horse over the landscape of their slumbering bodies.

Frankie shoved aside her worries and returned to the task at hand. Namely, wiping down the counters with disinfectant spray. "Day off" was a misnomer. She might not be going into the café, but she'd be working, all right. Doing laundry. Vacuuming. Unclogging that slow drain in the hall bathroom. Mending torn pajamas.

There was also her catering business. Ronnie had given Frankie's name to a friend who was throwing a giant anniversary bash in a few weeks. Then there was Mel and Aaron's upcoming wedding reception. Frankie should start researching the best prices for meat and supplies. If she found a deal, she'd buy what she could and store everything in her dad's giant chest freezer.

Hearing her cell phone ring, she returned the spray bottle to its place beneath the sink. Though expected, the name and number on the display still sent an electric shock through her from head to toe.

She quickly checked on the girls before pressing the phone to her ear. "Hello, Spence."

"Morning." He paused. "I was wondering…"

"Yes?"

"I'd like to come over and continue our conversation from last night."

She glanced again at the girls, who sang along with a song on the DVD they'd heard a hundred times.

"Um." The timing wasn't great. But if she refused him, he might accuse her of being uncooperative. "Sure. When were you thinking?"

"Now?"

She debated the many chores waiting her. Considered the toys scattered throughout the family room. Contemplated the dirty dishes she'd yet to load in the dishwasher.

Well, Spence would simply have to learn that maintaining a tidy house with two three-year-olds wasn't always possible.

"Give me thirty minutes." The very next second, her doorbell rang, rousing the dogs and sending them into a barking frenzy. "Hold on. Someone's here." She hurried to the front door, the dogs charging ahead of her. There, she peered through the peephole and groaned in frustration. "Seriously?" Disconnecting from Spence, she turned the knob, threw open the door and stared at him. "What are you doing?" she demanded. "You were supposed to call first."

"Like I said." He also disconnected and pocketed his phone. "We need to talk."

"I asked for thirty minutes."

"I was in the neighborhood."

Only because he'd intended to ambush her. Before she could accuse him, she bit her tongue. He might well say she'd done the same thing last night.

"Can I come in?" He quirked one corner of his mouth.

In the past, that move would have melted her fiercest determination like ice on a hot stove. Apparently, she was as weak as ever, for she stepped aside.

"Be my guest."

He wiped his boots on the welcome mat before entering and removed his hat. Recognizing someone they'd met the previous evening, the dogs immediately lost interest after a good sniffing and wandered off. Only then did Frankie notice Spence carried a paper bag.

"Bearing gifts?" she asked dubiously.

"More like a bribe." He reached into the bag and produced a carton of ice cream. "I hope everyone likes chocolate and caramel."

"It's a little early for junk food."

"Trust me, there's nothing junky about ice cream."

Naturally, he'd chosen her favorite flavor. "I'll put it away for later." She accepted the carton and led him to the kitchen, noting that his gaze went to the girls watching TV in the adjoining family room.

When they glanced up, he gave them a tentative smile. "Morning. Paige and Sienna, right?" He pointed to each one, correctly identifying them.

They nodded in unison but remained cautiously mute. Frankie started to reintroduce them, only to clamp her mouth shut. What should she say? "Girls, you remember Spence? Mr. Bohanan? Your father?" Oh, God. She should have thought this through more. Come up with a better plan. Any plan.

Did he realize how much Sienna resembled him? While Paige was a miniature version of Frankie and her sisters—a blond-haired, brown-eyed pixie—Sienna had inherited Spence's height and darker features. Frankie saw him every time she looked at Sienna. Did he?

Paige, always the more outgoing of the two, scrambled to her feet and bounded over. "Why are you here?"

"I came to visit you." Spence rounded the breakfast bar, pulled out a stool and patted it, inviting Paige to sit. She did, and he joined her, settling his large frame on the small stool next to hers. "Brought some ice cream, but your mom says you have to wait."

"Ice cream!" Paige turned pleading eyes on Frankie. "Can we have some, Mommy? Please?"

"In a while."

"But we're hungry." She included her sister, a tactic she employed to improve her odds of getting what she wanted.

"How about some apples and milk."

"Chocolate milk?"

Spence drew back and stared at Paige with admiration. "You're quite the negotiator."

"What's a ne-go-sur-a-tor?"

"Someone who's always finagling for more," Frankie answered.

"What's fi-na-ga…" She gave up, uttering a very grown-up sound of disgust.

"Plain milk." Frankie was already going to the refrigerator for apples and the carton of milk.

Paige knew she'd been bested. That didn't stop her from shooting Spence a mischievous grin. In turn, he winked and gave her a thumbs-up.

Frankie went still, the room starting to spin. How could she not have noticed before how much alike they were? Paige may not resemble him, but she and Spence were two peas in a pod.

"You okay, Mommy?"

She blinked. Steadied herself. "Yeah, sweetie. Just thinking." Grabbing an apple, she shut the refrigerator door. Good. Something to keep her busy. She dug in the drawer for a knife.

By now, Sienna had crept over, not wanting to be excluded from the potential fun. She climbed onto the last remaining bar stool, the one beside Paige, and peeked around her sister.

"You like ice cream, too?" Spence asked.

She nodded silently.

"What's your favorite game?"

"Animal hospital!" Paige threw her hands up in the air.

"Yours, too?" he asked Sienna, who nodded in reply. "Do you practice on the dogs?"

"No." Paige broke into riotous laughter. "They chew off the bandages."

"I've chewed off a bandage or two myself."

Sienna stared at him with owl-eyed wonder.

Paige was less gullible. "No, you haven't," she insisted.

Frankie finished slicing the apple. Setting a

plate with the snack in front of the girls, she then poured two glasses of milk. How they could be hungry, she didn't know. Her stomach felt like a cannonball sat in the middle. Then again, they had no idea who Spence really was.

Once the twins each snared an apple slice, Spence helped himself to one.

"Hey!" Paige objected, though Frankie could tell by her tone that she wasn't really mad.

Frankie watched the three of them interacting while she loaded the dishwasher. Was he forming a genuine connection with her daughters or just being his usual fun-loving, charming self?

"Your mom says you go to preschool. You like it?" he asked.

"No." Paige frowned while Sienna nodded enthusiastically.

"What about horses? You like them?"

"Yes!" For the first time, Sienna joined in, babbling, "I want a pony, but Mommy says no."

She was like her father in that regard, it seemed, unable to get enough of horses and riding.

"Someday, maybe," Frankie said.

"I have an idea," Spence announced. "My mares are arriving this afternoon. The driver's delivering them to Powell Ranch. Since you're off work—" he indicated Frankie "—and the girls don't have preschool, why don't we all go? You can see the mares and the girls can play with the other horses."

Naturally, Paige and Sienna responded enthusiastically, bouncing on their stools and nearly spilling their milk.

"I don't know," Frankie hedged. "They're only three."

"Almost four," Paige corrected her.

"Come on," Spence said. "It'll give me a chance to get to know these two better."

Frankie held her breath, waiting for him to say "my daughters." Fortunately, he simply tugged on Paige's hair and grinned at Sienna.

"Please, please, please, Mommy," they chorused.

Frankie wanted to say no. This was hard

enough. Going out in public as a family? She didn't think she was ready.

"What time?" she asked.

Apparently, Spence and the girls all took her question as agreeing, for they cheered and whooped.

"Pick up your toys first, or no one's going anywhere."

Realizing she had indeed given in, she let out a long, weary sigh.

Chapter Five

Powell Ranch bustled with activity, considering it was a weekday and still rather warm outside. Riders exercised their horses in the arena, the farrier trimmed the hooves of a skittish young foal and a trio of tourists readied for a guided trail ride.

Spence strolled the grounds with Ethan Powell, head horse trainer and one of the brothers who owned and operated the ranch. The family had gained quite a reputation in recent years, the result of capturing Prince, a former wild mustang and descendent of the original herd that gave the area its name.

As a result, the family had founded a non-profit mustang sanctuary—recently relocated to The Small Change Ranch—and made a name for themselves breeding, raising and training either rehabilitated mustangs or Prince's offspring.

"Any chance I can see Prince?" Spence asked. They'd just come from the main horse stables, where he'd checked out the stalls for the pregnant mares.

"Sure." Ethan flashed an easy grin. He was probably asked the question a lot. "He has his own setup behind the stables."

Ethan was a few years older than Spence and walked with a noticeable limp. Spence had heard the story of the marine veteran, how he'd lost his leg during a tour in the Middle East. Returning home after his medical discharge, he'd refused to let his disability end his rodeo career and went on to show the world he could still bust broncs.

His instinct for instantly spotting the best and worst in a horse was well known and respected. Spence thought he could learn a thing or two from Ethan, even though they trained different kinds of horses.

"Here we are," Ethan said with obvious pride, when they entered Prince's domain.

"Pretty damn nice."

Calling the two connected buildings a "setup" was a gross understatement. The facility consisted of a state-of-the-art breeding shed and spacious, fully-equipped mini stables for Prince and whatever lady friend he happened to be entertaining at the moment.

The strikingly colored mustang snorted in greeting and rushed the stall door the moment he spied Spence and Ethan.

"Hey, pal." Ethan patted the big stallion's muscular neck.

Rather than display the fiery temper one might expect, Prince behaved like a puppy dog, nuzzling Ethan and nickering softly. When Ethan produced a carrot from his pocket, the stallion gobbled it up, and then bumped Ethan's arm in a bid for more.

"That's all, big fellow."

"He's impressive." Spence waited, gauging the stallion's reaction to him. After receiving no more than a curious glance, he closed the distance between them and reached out a tentative hand. "I can see why he's in constant demand."

"I hear tell you're in the stud business, too," Ethan said.

"Not like you. I only own a small percentage."

"I researched Han Dover Fist and Cottonwood Farms after you contacted me about leasing stalls. Quite a success story."

"It is." Spence opened his palm for Prince to sniff. Disappointed not to find a treat, the stallion looked away as if he couldn't be bothered. "Some days, I still pinch myself."

"Are your mares bred to Han Dover Fist?"

"No. I wish they were. Maybe next time. But the sire has a pretty solid record, both on the track and for producing winning colts. I got the mares for a great price. Their former owner ran into some unforeseen financial trouble."

"I suppose that happens a lot in horse racing."

Frankie's words came back to Spence. As a single man with few responsibilities, he'd been willing to take calculated risks with his money. Now, he could understand her hesitancy, even to start a home-based business. Children changed everything. At the reminder of Paige and Sienna, his heart began to hammer inside his chest. It was a regular occurrence since learning he was a father. Not a panic attack exactly. More like acute nerves.

He and Frankie really needed to talk and reach an agreement, though what that agreement would be, he had no idea. The whole "I'm a dad," and everything it entailed, hadn't fully sunk in. Was he expected to share custody? Would she rather he went away and left them alone? How would she react if he asked to take the girls to meet his family in Marana?

Wow. His family. What would they say? Spence had yet to tell them, needing a day to come to terms with his unexpected fatherhood. His parents would be thrilled—they loved his brother's children. But they would probably like it better if Spence was married to his daughters' mother.

Marriage. Another consideration. Did Frankie want him to propose? Should he?

Spence thought he might be a little happy about his sudden parenthood. Paige and Sienna were certainly cute and very precocious, each in her own way. But was he ready for all the responsibilities that came with being a father? A husband? Spence could admit that the notion gave him considerable pause.

"How far along are they?"

Ethan's question snapped Spence back to the present. He almost said "three years old" before realizing the other man was referring to the pregnant state of his mares and not his daughters' ages.

"One's due in January, the other in February. My vet examined them before the trip, and they're progressing well."

"When they're closer to delivery, we can move them to the maternity stalls. Those are located in the building next door." Ethan gave Prince a last scratch before moving away. "If you're still here."

Did no one believe Spence capable of putting down roots?

Ethan finished showing him around the breeding shed and maternity stalls. After that, they toured the riding arena, training pens, outdoor stalls, pastures and feed storage barns. Spence was thoroughly impressed. No wonder Powell Ranch was considered one of the top horse stables in southern Arizona.

He had something to aspire to, though the racing quarter horse farm of his dreams was a bit smaller. For starters. Having a family to support provided even greater incentive and gave wings to his dreams.

Family. As in children and a wife. His goal, along with a racing horse farm, had been to win back Frankie. Now, after learning she'd lied to him for years, he found his feelings had changed.

She should have told him. Though past being angry, he was still hurt. Had she thought so little of him? Spence might have been bitten by the wandering bug, was a little loose when it came to rules and had a chronic hole in his pocket, but he wasn't a complete washup. Not then and certainly not now.

When Ethan's phone chimed, he excused himself. "You okay on your own?"

"No worries." Spence waved the other man off. "The transport truck's due in about fifteen minutes." Which reminded him. Where were Frankie and the girls?

Spence wandered back to the open area outside the ranch office. From there, he had a clear view of the long, winding drive leading from the main road and up the mountain to the ranch.

He'd wanted to swing by Frankie's house on his way here, but she'd insisted on driving separately. Agreeing was a concession, the first of many, Spence figured. He and Frankie would have to learn to navigate this new relationship of theirs. Arguing over driving together or separately was no way to start.

Just when he'd removed his phone to text her, he spotted her minivan slowly climbing the drive. Checking the time, he smiled to himself. Now who was five minutes late?

She swung the vehicle into the empty space beside his truck. He strode briskly over, reaching the driver's side door just as Frankie emerged.

"Hi. You're here." He didn't comment on her late arrival. Her serious expression didn't invite teasing.

"Paige couldn't find her shoes." She opened the rear passenger door. "Did we miss the transport truck?"

The girls sat in identical car seats and wore similar pants and tops. Did everything they own match? Was that a requirement for twins? Well, at least they didn't look alike. Spence wouldn't have trusted himself to tell them apart if they were identical.

"Nope," he said. "Should be here any minute."

He watched, fascinated, as Frankie unfastened what seemed like an inordinate number of buckles and snaps to free the girls. First Paige, then Sienna, bounded out of the vehicle.

"Mommy, can we pet the horses?"

"I wanna go riding. Please, please, please."

"Now, now," Frankie answered in a calm voice. "We can look at the horses and maybe pet them. We can't ride any."

"We could. If they want," Spence continued, when Frankie shot him an annoyed look. "The stables rent horses by the hour. They have plenty suitable for kids. Ethan told me."

"We're not riding today," she repeated. When the girls would have run off in two different directions, she grabbed their hands and anchored them in place.

"Another day then," Spence said. "My treat."

"We'll see. They're kind of young."

"I'd like to take them riding, Frankie. Even if it's just in the arena. I'm sure the Powells can recommend a dead-broke mount. I promise we'll only walk."

"Can we just look at the horses today? Maybe pet some of the gentler ones?"

There was a nervousness in her tone he hadn't heard before. Was he the cause or an overactive maternal instinct to protect her children? Whatever the reason, he decided to respect her wishes.

"Let's visit the stables first. I can show you the stalls I'm leasing for the mares while we're waiting for the transport truck. And I'm sure there's a few horses eager for the attention of these two."

Frankie instantly relaxed, and they began walking, with Spence leading the way.

"I'm not overreacting," she said. "This past spring, Dad took the girls riding double on an old ranch horse belonging to the McGraws."

Spence recognized the name. The McGraws owned The Small Change Ranch, where Frankie's father worked as livestock manager, and the mustang sanctuary was located.

"Twenty minutes into the ride," she continued, "the horse spooked at a rattlesnake hidden behind a rock, and the girls fell off. Not near the snake, thank goodness, and they weren't hurt, other than a few bumps and bruises. But they were scared, and I was terrified. They haven't been on a horse since."

"We can go slow." Spence had started riding when he was younger than Paige and Sienna and didn't see the problem. He wouldn't push, however. Not yet.

"We'll see," Frankie repeated.

She was setting boundaries. Right from the get-go. Okay, he could deal with that. He might eventually set a few of his own, once he'd gained more experience at this parenting stuff.

Today, however, was all about getting to know Paige and Sienna and them getting to know him—something he was looking forward to more than he would have thought possible.

"PAIGE. SIENNA. COME back here. Right this second. I'm warning you."

Spence could hear the frustration in Frankie's voice. See it on her face. Feel it pouring off her in waves.

They'd been inside the horse stables for ten minutes at most and already the girls had run off three different times, getting as far as the end of the aisle on their latest venture.

Laughing, they reluctantly returned to the empty stall where Spence and Frankie stood. Sienna showed no fear around the horses, reaching out to stroke every curious nose she passed, even when Frankie warned her to be careful.

Secretly, Spence admired her courage. "She's a natural."

His remark didn't please Frankie, earning him a scowl.

Living up to his assessment, Sienna abruptly stopped in front of a young gelding which had been nervously pacing within the confines of his stall since they'd entered the stables.

"No, Sienna!" Frankie started forward, clearly intending to rescue her daughter from the clutches of danger.

Spence took hold of her arm. "Wait."

The horse stopped pacing and leaned his impressive head over the stall door, low enough to smell Sienna.

"What did I tell you?" Spence said, as the animal stood while Sienna patted his face and cooed. "A natural."

Frankie shot him another scowl.

"She reminds me of my brother's daughter." He'd been trying to figure out what it was about Sienna that seemed familiar to him.

"She reminds me of you. She has your features."

Did she? Spence studied her more closely, trying to see the resemblance.

A distant rumbling sound distracted them. "They're here," he announced.

The arrival of the transport truck was further confirmed by two short bursts of a low horn. Frankie rounded up the girls, and the four of them went out to watch the truck's arrival.

Spence was aware of the glances cast in their direction. From Ethan's wife, who'd brought her husband a cold drink. From the nosy older woman he'd met twice yesterday, here and again at the café. And from riders in the arena.

If people weren't sure before today that he was Paige and Sienna's father, they most certainly were now. Spence ignored their scrutiny. While still getting used to the idea of having children, he saw no reason to be embarrassed or feel guilty.

Neither, apparently, did Frankie. Then again, if the stories Spence had heard were to be believed, she'd been ignoring the stares for years.

Well, good for her. It couldn't have been easy, refusing to name the father of her children. No doubt one or two unkind people had criticized her.

The large truck and trailer rolled slowly into the yard and stopped in front of the office. A small crowd instantly gathered, oohing and ahhing and gasping in admiration. Spence felt a little awed himself. Luxury transport trucks were a sight to behold.

Sunlight glinted off the trailer's chrome siding, the bright glare blinding. Horses' heads bobbed up and down behind the enclosed Plexiglas windows. An air-conditioning unit mounted atop the trailer chugged noisily.

Spence grinned, his excitement growing. "Come on."

"We'll wait here," Frankie answered.

No problem. He'd bring the mares to her and the girls.

As he approached the truck, the driver's side door opened, and a short, stout, jovial man emerged. Pausing with one foot on the running board, he issued a friendly "Howdy," before tucking in his wrinkled shirt and jumping down.

"Have any more trouble?" Spence shook the man's hand.

"Not once we got past the flooding in Texas." The driver led Spence toward the rear of the trailer, where he unlocked and swung open the gate. He then lowered the ramp, which hit the ground with a dull clank. "These pretty ladies traveled just fine. But they're glad to be at their new home."

Spence inspected the first mare as she was unloaded, noting she'd endured the arduous three-day journey with few ill effects. He held her lead rope while the driver unloaded the second mare. She also passed inspection. Nonetheless, he'd have them checked out by a veterinarian as soon as possible.

They, and the foals they carried, were too important to his future plans. Plans that had taken on new importance now that he was a father.

Frankie and the girls weren't the only ones to accompany Spence and the mares to the stalls. Ethan, his wife and several onlookers followed, offering their compliments on the long-legged, sleek-coated beauties.

Once each mare was safely settled in her stall with fresh water and hay, Spence signed off on the paperwork and paid the remaining funds due. He offered to buy the driver dinner at the café, but the man was more interested in getting back on the road.

People stayed to watch the big truck and trailer leave, clapping like spectators at a parade as it circled the stables before driving through the ranch gate.

Frankie joined Spence at the stalls. "Quite a show."

"You got me figured out. My goal all along was to impress you."

"I am impressed. But not by what you think."

"Do tell."

"You haven't left Mustang Valley. I thought I might have scared you off."

"Oh, I'm scared," he admitted. "Make no mistake. Those two kids have me quaking in my boots."

"They can do that. To me, too." She leaned back to scrutinize him. "But just because you've impressed me, don't let it go to your head."

"Too late. In fact, I'm surprised my hat still fits."

"You're impossible." Flirty laughter laced her voice, reminding him of when they were dating.

It came to an abrupt end when Paige ran up to Spence and tugged on his shirt.

He looked down to meet her inquisitive gaze. "Hey, there."

"What's your name?"

Spence swallowed. Frankie paled.

This moment was bound to happen. They should have discussed what to say beforehand and come up with an answer that would satisfy the girls without revealing too much, too soon. Only they hadn't.

By now, Sienna had also come over. She stood beside her sister, waiting expectantly.

"Um, okay." Nothing like being put on the spot. He cleared his throat. "Most folks call me Spence."

"That's a funny name." Paige pressed splayed fingers to her mouth to hide her laughter.

To Spence's consternation, Frankie offered no assistance whatsoever.

"It's short for Spencer," he said. "I'm named after my grandfather."

Sienna apparently lost interest, for she asked, "Can I pet your horses?"

Spence relaxed. Disaster had been narrowly averted. For the moment, anyway.

"Sure." He lifted her up so that she could give the nearest mare plenty of attention.

This one, with an irregular white diamond in the center of her face, abandoned her feed bin in order to investigate the young human intruder. Her quiet disposition, and that of the other mare, was a major selling point. Fiery temperaments weren't necessary to win races. A will to run was what really mattered.

Spence felt Frankie's gaze on him. What, he wondered, was she thinking? That he didn't know the first thing about children and would probably drop Sienna? Maybe Frankie was struggling to accept the idea of him interacting with her daughters. *Their* daughters.

Well, it was a new experience for him, too. A little uncomfortable and awkward at times. Interesting and enjoyable at others. Like now.

"Do you think Mel might be willing to examine the mares for me?" he asked Frankie.

"Probably." She pulled out her phone. "I'll text you her number."

"Great." After Sienna had her fill and asked to be put down, he offered Paige a turn.

She shook her head vigorously and wrinkled her nose. "Horses smell bad."

Spence laughed. "What kind of Har—" He'd been about to say Hartman. But she was every bit a Bohanan. Shrugging a shoulder, he suggested, "Maybe we can change your mind."

Her response was another head shake. Grabbing Sienna's hand, she asked, "Mommy, can we play hide-and-seek?"

"You need to stay where I can see you."

Paige pouted. "How can we hide?"

Frankie wagged a finger at her. "You heard me."

The pair scurried off to where a saddle sat on a sawhorse outside the tack room, waiting to be cleaned or repaired. Immediately, Sienna attempted to boost Paige onto the saddle.

"You mind if I look these two over?" He hitched a thumb at the mares.

"You mind if I watch?"

"Not at all."

It was a lot like old times, him riding or tending his horses and her watching. She had to remember, as well.

"You've done a wonderful job raising Paige and Sienna."

He entered the stall of the bay mare. Holding out a hand to calm her, he then ran his palm along her side, feeling the slight swell of her flank beneath which the foal rested. Did Mel have ultrasound equipment? He'd ask when he called.

Probing the mare's leg for any swelling or tenderness, he said, "It can't always be easy for you."

"It isn't, but I manage. Dad's a big help. And now Dolores. She loves the girls, and they're fond of her."

"That's nice. When were they born, by the way?"

"They'll be four on December 3." Her spine straightened. "That's eight months after you left the last time, in case you're doing the math."

"Hey, don't get mad. I'm just curious."

Satisfied with the mare's condition, Spence left the stall, planning on giving his other mare the same meticulous attention.

Frankie put a hand on his arm as he passed her. "I'm sorry. I shouldn't have been short with you. It's reasonable for you to wonder. If you are, that is. You've been gone a long time, and I didn't contact you when I learned I was pregnant."

He softened his voice. "I'm not wondering, Frankie."

"All right." She nodded. "That's good."

He searched her face. Leaned slowly in as if pulled by an undeniable attraction. Back when they were dating, he'd have taken a moment like this to steal a kiss. He didn't now, certain she'd resist, what with their daughters close by, but that didn't diminish the sudden desire coursing through him.

"I should…find the girls." Collecting herself, she withdrew her hand and effectively ended the moment.

"Sure." He didn't protest. It was enough to know the sparks were still there.

He'd barely unlocked the latch on the other mare's stall when Frankie's cries had him whirling around.

"They're gone!"

"What?"

"Paige and Sienna. They've disappeared." She glanced frantically about. "They were playing with the saddle a minute ago." She started toward the sawhorse.

Spence hurried after her. "Where would they go?"

"I don't know." Her voice had risen a full octave and panic filled her eyes. "I should have been paying better attention. This is my fault."

"If anyone's to blame, it's me. I distracted you."

"They've done this before. Run off when my

back was turned. They think it's funny and don't realize they're giving me a heart attack."

Heart attack? That must explain the explosive pounding inside Spence's chest. He could hardly breathe.

Striving to remain calm, he said, "They can't be far."

"Do you think they could have gotten in with one of the horses?"

"I doubt it." He scanned the length of the aisle. "Most of the stalls have padlocks on the doors."

"We should check."

"You do that." He noticed the tack room door was ajar. "I'll look in here."

Frankie immediately darted from stall to stall, glancing inside and alarming the horses, who snorted and tossed their heads in annoyance.

Spence pushed open the tack room door, flipped the light switch and waited for his eyes to adjust. The smell of leather combined with floating dust particles tickled his nose. He searched in the direction of scuffling noises but didn't see anything. Probably one of the barn cats or even some mice.

"Hello." He checked behind the racks holding long lengths of harnesses. "Paige? Sienna? You here?"

The sound of muffled giggling was unmistakable.

He hurried to the door and hollered, "Frankie. I found them."

"Thank God." She came running back.

Two minutes later, she was brushing dirt and dust off the girls' clothes and admonishing them for running off when she'd specifically told them to stay where she could see them.

How could she be so calm? Spence's heart still raced a mile a minute, and his shirt was drenched in sweat.

He stared at Paige and Sienna, trying to make sense of his reaction. Was this what it felt like to be a parent? Intense worry one second and overwhelming relief the next?

If so, he'd taken his first steps.

Chapter Six

Earlier today, Frankie had imagined how the afternoon would unfold. She'd predicted a certain amount of stress, along with awkwardness and discomfort. Best case scenario, they'd survive emotionally unscathed and try again. Never, ever, had she expected Spence, Paige and Sienna to get along like…a father and his children.

He was good with them. Great, actually. When the girls went missing, Spence had reacted quickly. When they were found, she'd been touched by his obvious relief.

Why, then, was she feeling confused and a little annoyed instead of happy?

Standing on the steps to the office, she watched them play fetch with one of the many ranch dogs. From the level of the girls' excitement, one would think they didn't have two dogs of their own at home that regularly chased balls.

The reason must be Spence. Did Paige and Sienna instinctively sense on some level that he was their father?

No. Impossible. Bonds required time and close contact to form, right? The girls simply liked the attention he was paying them, which must account for why they hadn't glanced once in her direction for the last twenty minutes.

Frankie rubbed her temple where a small throb persisted. Examining Spence's budding relationship with the girls was impossible without also examining his relationship with her. He'd returned to Mustang Valley in order to rekindle their former romance. Yeah, yeah, to start a racing horse farm, but for her, too. He'd made that clear.

Had he changed his mind? Last night, he'd kissed her, and with a fair amount of passion. When they were standing at the horse stalls, their conversation had verged on intimate, and she'd wondered if he might kiss her again.

Since finding the girls in the tack room, however, he'd focused entirely on them, and they, in turn, on him. Frankie might as well not even be there.

My God! Was she jealous? Frankie had to ponder that for a moment. Up until now, there'd been no one to compete with her for the twins' affection. Not that Frankie and Spence were in a competition.

She was merely getting used to the change in family dynamics. Yes, that was it.

He tossed the ball for the umpteenth time. When the dog gave chase, the girls erupted with excitement. Frankie sighed. This could be a heartwarming scene from a Hallmark movie, other than the fact she wasn't included.

Once, she'd been head over heels in love with Spence. After he left and she recovered from the hurt, she'd assigned him the place in her heart reserved for a onetime boyfriend who also happened to be the father of her children.

But now he was back, and possibly had his sights set on her. Could she love him again, the way she had before? Frankie didn't know.

One giant obstacle lay between them, and it was called trust. He'd have to earn hers before she'd take the leap again. His growing affection for Paige and Sienna was a start, she supposed. A small start.

The next moment, Frankie spotted a white pickup truck pulling into the ranch, its familiar RodeoGal vanity license plate on the front announcing the arrival of Ronnie and Sam.

She waited for her sisters while they parked in the designated area behind the stables. "Girls," she called. "Aunt Ronnie and Sam are here."

In response, Spence waved. Paige and Sienna ignored her.

That hadn't happened since Santa Claus "visited" their preschool. They were mama's girls, as Frankie's dad was fond of saying. Frankie had always secretly delighted in the remark, liking that she mattered most in the world to her daughters.

The twinge of jealously she insisted she wasn't feeling pricked her hard. She told herself this afternoon was simply a new and different experience. Paige and Sienna would be mama's girls again as soon as they arrived home.

Her sisters strolling casually toward the office steps were a welcome distraction. This soul-searching stuff was wearing on Frankie.

"Hey, I didn't know you two would be here."

"I told you last night," Sam said, pausing at the bottom step.

"Did you?" Frankie had forgotten amid all the excitement today. Truth be told, from the second she'd discovered Spence sitting at the café counter, she'd been suffering from memory lapses.

"Today is Sam's last chance to practice," Ronnie said. "We're leaving in the morning for Lancaster."

That was right. Sam was competing in the California Circuit Finals. With luck, she'd end her recent bad luck streak.

Frankie would have to find another babysitter for tomorrow during those few hours between when preschool was over and her shift at work ended.

She considered Spence, but immediately quashed the notion. Too much too soon. They needed to start slow. And besides, he was busy during the day with his mares and whatever was involved with starting a racing quarter horse farm.

The throb in her temple resumed. "Are Dad and Dolores going with you?" she asked Ronnie.

"Only Dad. Dolores isn't supposed to put any weight on her foot for another couple weeks."

Ah, yes. Her stepmom's minor surgery. Something else that had slipped Frankie's mind. Her list of potential babysitters was dwindling at an alarming rate.

"Is that him?" Sam pointed at Spence.

"A little less obvious, please," Frankie admonished. "And, yes, that's Spence."

She'd told Sam about Spence. She didn't have much choice; the teenager was living with her, after all. But Sam had been warned to keep her mouth shut in front of the twins until Frankie gave her the go ahead—which, if Spence got his way, would be soon.

The thought of telling her daughters caused a knot to form in Frankie's stomach. How would they respond? What if they were angry at her for lying, just like Spence had been, if not still was?

Sam openly stared at him. "You didn't mention how hot he is."

Frankie frowned. "He's way too old for you!"

"I'm just looking. No harm in that."

Ronnie peered over Sam's shoulder. "We're all just looking." At Frankie's deepening frown, she said, "Quit your worrying. He's interested in you and you alone. Been that way for the last fifteen years."

Frankie straightened her spine. She couldn't

care less that other women checked out Spence. It wasn't as if they were seeing each other or had an agreement.

Changing the subject, she asked, "Shouldn't you two be practicing or something?"

Neither sister moved.

"He's a natural with Paige and Sienna," Ronnie commented, shading her eyes from the sun.

"They like dogs."

"They like him."

Frankie refused to admit having the identical thought mere minutes before.

"Are you going to keep him around?" Sam asked, her voice at the same embarrassingly loud level.

"Not my decision. He may be staying. He may leave. His choice."

"Can I meet him?"

"Well, um…" She supposed there was no avoiding the inevitable. "I guess."

Suddenly, everyone's attention was diverted to another truck and trailer pulling into the ranch. This one wasn't nearly as big or impressive as the luxury transport truck delivering Spence's mares.

"Is that Cara Dempsey?" Frankie asked, recognizing the mustang sanctuary manager.

Ronnie started down the steps. "She's bringing a few horses by for Ethan to assess and possibly train. The adoption event is less than two weeks away."

At least twice each year, the mustang sanctuary put on a community-wide event that brought in supporters from all over the state and as far away as Colorado and New Mexico. The goal was to find homes for the tamer mustangs and to raise money for the sanctuary by auctioning off donated items. In addition, raffle tickets were sold for a particularly good-looking mustang that showed immense promise.

Cara's truck drew nearer. Before Frankie could holler for Paige and Sienna to get out of the way, Spence grabbed one squealing twin in each arm and carried them to safety, tucked close to his sides like a pair of footballs.

Frankie simply stared. Did daughters need

their father? She'd always assumed her guidance and influence would be enough. What if she was wrong?

"Are you okay?" Ronnie asked. "You look a little frazzled."

"Just a headache." A whopper.

All three sisters made their way to Spence and the girls. Sam didn't wait for an introduction.

"Hi." She beamed at him. "I'm Samantha."

He tugged on the brim of his cowboy hat. "Nice to meet you, Sam. I've heard a lot about you."

While they chatted, Frankie gathered up the girls. They were less than enthused.

She bent down in order to put her face on their level. "Ready to go home?"

"No-o-o!" they cried in unison, their babbled reasons for wanting to stay drowning each other out.

"Okay, okay. But only for a little while longer."

At this point, Ethan and Spence wandered over to help Cara unload the horses and give them a closer look. Frankie had absorbed enough equine knowledge from her other family members to see that these three, while not gorgeous, were solid, sturdy stock and would probably bring in a decent amount of money at the adoption event.

Ethan instructed Cara to put the mustangs in the outdoor stalls. She headed off, leading them with the same ease and competence she might have if walking a trio of puppies.

When Frankie next looked over at Spence, he and Ethan were engaged in what seemed like a serious conversation. Curious, she took the girls' hands and maneuvered closer in order to—okay, she admitted it—eavesdrop.

"Have you ever raced any of the mustangs?" Spence asked.

Race them? What was he thinking?

"No." Ethan laughed good-naturedly. "Never considered it, either."

"That buckskin gelding has some length on his legs. I think he might give my mares a run for their money."

"Not likely."

"Maybe we should give it a try one of these days. After my mares have delivered."

That wouldn't be until the first of next year. Was Spence implying he'd still be here three months from now?

"Mustangs are capable of surviving some pretty harsh terrain," Ethan said thoughtfully. "And they can outrun the fastest predators."

"Like I said." Spence grinned broadly. "You may have some racing stock."

"It did take four of us to capture Prince. He put up a heck of a fight."

"Have you ever clocked him?" Spence asked.

"No reason."

Frankie couldn't believe her eyes and ears. These two were getting along as if they'd been buddies for years. To her further astonishment, within the next minute, they were hatching a plan to race Prince across the arena. For fun, of course. Just to see how fast he was.

"I don't have a racing saddle," Ethan said.

"I do. In my truck."

"You want to ride him?"

"Nah." Spence shook his head. "I'm too heavy. We need someone smaller. Lighter."

"I'll do it!" Sam piped up. She'd obviously been listening to the conversation, too.

"Have you ever ridden a racehorse?"

"No, but I'm a barrel racer. I run horses at a full gallop every day."

Spence's grin grew. "Good enough for me."

There was no reason Frankie couldn't, or shouldn't, load the girls into her vehicle and head home. Except now, bad joke aside, wild horses couldn't drag her away.

FRANKIE STOOD AT the fence on the south end of the arena, along with about two dozen other spectators, including her sister Ronnie, Ethan Powell and Cara Dempsey. Beside her, Spence played with a stopwatch.

On her other side, the twins alternately sifted through the loose dirt for pebbles and draped themselves over the lowest fence railing. Frankie wasn't convinced they fully understood what was happening. They only knew that Sam was going to ride a big horse really fast down the length of the arena.

Frankie's gaze went to Sam, who sat atop Prince at the opposite end. Two ranch hands were busy clearing away barrels, poles and orange training cones in preparation of the mini race. Despite never riding the stallion before, or sitting in the tiny scrap of leather Spence called a racing saddle, the teenager appeared completely at ease. Prince also looked as if he couldn't be bothered by all the fuss. Lowering his head, he rubbed his nose on his front leg, probably to relieve an itch.

"You ready?" Spence hollered to Sam, when the ranch hands signaled they were done.

She waved in reply and readied herself by leaning forward over Prince's neck and elevating the lower half of her body.

Spence had given her a few pointers beforehand, expressing confidence in her abilities. Frankie worried nonetheless. The stallion was big. Sam was small and young and inexperienced when it came to racing.

"What if she gets hurt?"

"She'll be fine," Spence absently replied, his eyes glued to Sam and Prince.

Wasn't that just like a guy? Frankie's father had said the same thing right before they took the twins riding. Then the horse had spooked at a rattlesnake, and the girls ended up hurt and scared.

"Shouldn't Ethan be in there with her?" She chewed on a thumbnail. "Something could go wrong."

"We don't want Prince's attention on anyone else except Sam."

"Go, Sam, go!" Sienna shouted in her high-pitched voice.

Great. Frankie's usually subdued daughter had suddenly developed a pair of lungs.

"All set." Spence lifted his free hand high in the air. At once, everyone went still, including—and this was a minor miracle—Paige and Sienna.

Sam watched Spence with unwavering concentration. Frankie watched Sam, her heart seeming to stop beating.

Spence's arm swiftly fell. Sam spurred Prince. The stallion came alive and charged ahead, going from a complete standstill to a full gallop in the span of a second.

"And, they're off!" Spence yelled.

Prince's hooves dug into the soft dirt as his churning legs became a blur. Sam gave him his head, and he extended his stride. Whoever said horses were incapable of expressing emotions was wrong. Frankie swore Prince's eyes burned with steely determination.

"Go, go, go!" she yelled, only to clamp a hand over her mouth.

Was this excitement coursing through her akin to what Spence had felt when he watched Han Dover Fist race? She didn't want to relate to him. Horse racing was an unreliable occupation.

Oh, what the heck. "Yes, yes." She shook her clenched fists. "That's it. Faster, faster."

Spence pressed a button on the stopwatch when Prince crossed in front of the white post, a marker they'd decided earlier would substitute for a finish line. He'd mentioned multiplying Prince's time by some formula to roughly approximate how the stallion would have performed if he'd run on a real track.

The spectators erupted in applause and cheers.

"She did it!" Frankie whirled on Spence. "That was fast."

He studied the stopwatch. "It was okay."

"Okay? They were flying."

"Taking into account they were running on loose dirt and not a packed track, I suppose it wasn't too terrible."

She stared at him. "You're wrong. Look again."

"Hey, don't be mad. They did good. For a couple of rookies."

Rookies? Frankie felt offended on Sam's behalf.

Having turned Prince around after passing the white post, the teenager now trotted him over. The enormous smile on her face said it all. She'd loved every moment.

"Look, he's not even winded." She patted Prince's neck.

"In a real race," Spence said, "he'd have run a full mile and be plenty winded.

Ethan sauntered over to join Spence. He also wore a smile. "How'd he do?"

Spence recited the final time, and they discussed the results compared to a real race.

"Respectable," Spence told him.

"But not fast enough for me to get into the racing business."

"Probably not."

"Still, it was fun there for a minute."

Spence clapped him on the shoulder. "No reason you can't have more fun, if you want."

Ethan's brows rose. "What are you suggesting?"

Frankie strained to hear what was being said while keeping the girls busy. With the race over, they'd begun to whine. Had they been home, she'd remedy their crankiness with a nap. Instead, she rummaged in her purse and, finding an emergency flashlight, gave it to them, hoping they'd amuse themselves.

"Pick out three or four of your best mustangs," Spence said. "Prince here can be one of them. Put on a mock race and sell tickets."

"To make money?" Ethan asked. "Is that legal?"

"For charity. Like at the adoption event you have coming up. I've seen it done before, fairly successfully. People place bets by buying tickets for a certain horse. Tickets for the winning horse are then redeemed for donated prizes. Everyone has a good time and you raise money for a worthy cause."

"I *love* the idea." Cara Dempsey stepped forward. In addition to managing the mustang sanctuary, she also headed up the adoption event. "I can see it working really well. I bet we could get media coverage." She turned to Spence, glowing with hope. "Will you help us?"

Frankie paused, anxiously awaiting his answer. Agreeing would require a commitment from him. To stay in Mustang Valley for the immediate future. To get involved. To volunteer his time and energy. Maybe he wasn't ready for all that. He had a lot going on.

One second dragged into two. *He's going to say no.* Frankie became convinced of it.

Exhaling slowly, he faced Cara.

Poor, poor Cara. She's going to be terribly disappointed.

"Be my pleasure to help." Spence flashed his best smile.

Really? His pleasure? Frankie blinked.

"I even have a couple of jockey friends I could probably recruit. You'd have to put them up for the weekend. Throw in a few meals."

"No problem." Cara clasped her hands together. "The Morning Side Inn is one of our sponsors. And I know of two horses I think would be perfect. The buckskin gelding with the scar on his hip." She nudged Ethan. "You know which one I'm talking about."

"I do. And I had that gray mare in mind."

"Yes! The escape artist. She's a born runner."

"We're going to need a track," Ethan mused.

"We could use the dirt road behind the cattle barns at The Small Change Ranch. Grade a long stretch with the tractor."

Cara and Ethan continued their discussion, heads bent together.

Sam hopped off the stallion in order to talk to Spence. "Can I ride Prince in the race?"

"I'm not his owner. That's up to Ethan."

"And if he says yes?"

Spence shrugged. "You'd need to train. And the adoption event is only a couple weeks off."

"I can train."

"What about your barrel racing?" Ronnie interjected. "Practice is every day. And you have a rodeo this weekend."

"I'll manage."

"No, you won't." Ronnie shook her head. "Not and still have time to watch Paige and Sienna."

Sam's features fell.

"Look," Spence said. "There's a lot that goes

into a mock race. Maybe we can all talk later. Come up with a plan of action."

"Good idea," Cara chimed in. "We should have a meeting. As soon as possible. Spence, are you free this weekend?"

"I suppose I could find the time."

"What about me?" Sam complained.

"We'll keep you posted," Cara assured her.

Frankie wanted to hear more, but the girls had reached their limit. Rather than amuse them, the small flashlight had become an object to fight over.

"We need to go." She bent and brushed dirt off the girls' shorts.

"I'll walk you to your van," Spence offered.

"Sure." Frankie had assumed he'd stay with Ethan and Cara and Sam.

Paige and Sienna behaved during the short walk to the minivan and, for once, willingly crawled into their car seats.

"They'll be asleep before we reach the main road," Frankie informed Spence.

"Thanks for coming."

"Thanks for inviting us. We had a good time. And your mares are beautiful." She briefly wondered if he'd try and kiss her, considering how close they'd come earlier in the horse stables, before the girls went missing.

"You think we can get together soon?" he asked. "We have a lot to talk about."

He certainly wasn't wasting any time. "Yes."

"When?"

She decided not to waste any time, either. "I have a full day tomorrow. How about tonight? You could come over for dinner. Say, six o'clock?" That would give her a couple hours to tidy the house and throw a meal together.

"We could go out."

"Obviously, you've never dined in a restaurant with two three-year-olds." She laughed softly. "I'll cook."

"I was hoping you'd say that."

Without any warning, he swept her up in a quick hug and gave her a peck on the cheek. "See you then."

Frankie had thought to throw him for a loop

by inviting him to dinner. So much for that. In fact, she was the one thrown—and liking the thrill much, much more than she should.

Chapter Seven

Spence had sat at a dinner table with children before. Frequently, while visiting his family in Marana. His brother's son and daughter were close in age to Paige and Sienna, he supposed, and also pretty darn cute.

But they weren't Spence's children. Eating a meal with *his* daughters was nothing short of mind-boggling.

"Hey, I said to stop that." Frankie scolded the girls yet again for sneaking green beans to the dogs. That triggered a string of protests.

"You'll have to excuse them," she said. "They've had a big day and didn't nap well."

She looked in need of a nap herself. Twice he'd seen her stifle a yawn, and her feet dragged when she served dinner. In hindsight, he should've insisted on eating out.

"Maybe—" he lowered his voice to a whisper "—some ice cream would help."

"Come on, girls." Frankie pointed to their plates. "Eat your green beans. If you finish them, you can have a dish of the ice cream Spen—" She stopped short of saying his name. "Ice cream for dessert."

They definitely needed to make some decisions. Tonight, if possible. Figure out when and how to tell the girls that he was their father. If only the twins and Frankie weren't so tired.

Spence tried to discreetly observe Paige and Sienna as they reluctantly swallowed microscopic bites of green beans. How would they react to the news? They seemed to like him. That was a good beginning, wasn't it? He liked them, too, far sooner than he'd thought possible.

They were young and would adapt quickly to the change. That was what his old boss had predicted when Spence called for advice. He'd also told Spence not to hurry the girls. Just be friendly and easygoing and allow them to warm up to him at their own pace.

Ice cream proved to be the magic cure for everyone. After choking down the last of their green beans, Paige and Sienna were rewarded with a small dish. Spence's dish contained a considerably larger serving.

He patted his stomach. "Don't know where I'm going to put this."

The girls mimicked him, to his great amusement.

"Say thank you," Frankie prompted.

"Thank you," Paige and Sienna chorused in unison, before scraping their dishes clean.

After dessert came bath time, a regular nightly ritual according to Frankie.

"Go on." Spence grabbed his dish and spoon. "I'll handle this."

"You?" She gaped at him as if he'd announced his intentions to run for president.

"I can wash dishes."

"Since when?"

"One of the many skills I've acquired over the years. For the record, I can also vacuum and launder my clothes."

"How come some lucky woman hasn't grabbed you up?" she teased.

His answer was anything but teasing. "We both know why that hasn't happened."

"Spence."

The girls abruptly scrambled from their chairs and asked if they could play.

"Bath first." Frankie propelled them down the hall, leaving him alone to clear the table and clean the kitchen.

What would she have said to him if they weren't interrupted? His imagination shifted into overdrive.

"Wow." Frankie stood in the entryway to the kitchen as he was finishing up some twenty minutes later, an approving expression on her face. "Nice job."

"I washed the platter by hand. Didn't think it should go in the dishwasher." He indicated the china platter sitting on the counter. "I wasn't sure where you put it."

She joined him at the sink and leaned in for a closer inspection. "You used scouring powder."

"My mom would have my hide if I left the sink and stove top dirty. She insisted I learn how to properly clean a kitchen."

Frankie straightened. "How are your parents, by the way?"

He smelled something flowery on her skin. Bubble bath, maybe? Or shampoo? Several blond strands lay against her cheek and neck, curling prettily. He was tempted to take one of those damp strands between his fingers and test its softness. Or bend his head and plant a light kiss beneath her ear, just to see if she'd push him away or lean in.

Instead, he said, "They're good. Dad owns the

dealership now. Bought out the owner a couple years ago and changed the name to Bohanan Auto Complex. Mom left her job at Southwest Hay Sales to run his office."

"That's great."

"I suspect my brother will take over one day."

"Not you?"

"Can you see me selling cars for a living?" He folded and rehung the dish towel.

"I suppose not." Mild amusement colored her voice. "What's your sister doing these days?"

"She moved to Seattle last year. Took a job with a winery in their marketing department."

"She like it?"

"I guess so." He shrugged. "She's dating the assistant winemaker."

"That's great. Sounds like everyone's doing well."

"They are. And the folks don't worry about me as much as they used to."

Frankie grew quiet. "I'm sure they're wonderful grandparents to your brother's children."

"That they are."

"I'm guessing you'd like to introduce them to…" She glanced over her shoulder. "The girls."

"Yes, I would. Eventually. Soon."

She nodded. "Have you told them?"

"I'm waiting to tell Paige and Sienna first. See how that goes. Where are they, by the way? In bed?"

"Playing in their room. I'll tuck them in shortly. It's back to preschool tomorrow, and I have an early shift."

Spence rested a hip on the counter. "I was wondering."

"Yes?" she prompted, when he hesitated.

"You'll probably think this is a strange request."

"What?"

"Do you have any baby pictures of the girls?"

Her curious expression gave way to one of surprise. "Lots. Are you kidding?"

"Can I see them? I'd like to know a little of what they were like as babies."

Frankie's features abruptly crumbled, and he thought she might cry.

"Are you okay?" He reached for her arm. "I didn't mean to upset you."

"I really am sorry, Spence. I believed I was doing the right thing by not telling you. At first. Truly. After a while, I started having doubts. But then…" She sniffed. "It got easier and easier as more time passed to talk myself out of telling you. Plus, I was afraid."

"Of what?"

"You being angry at me. Taking me to court. Suing for custody out of spite. I realize now I was wrong."

"I appreciate you saying that." He thought this was the most honest she'd been with him since his return. Because of that, he felt compelled to be honest with her. "I'm not sure I would have been the best father in the world if you'd told me at the start."

"But you deserved the chance."

"I have one now, and I'm going to try not to blow it."

Though no tears had fallen, she wiped at her cheeks. "Most of my pictures are digital. They're saved on my computer and cloud storage. I could transfer them to a portable thumb drive for you if you want. One for your parents, too."

"That'd be great. Thanks."

"In the meantime, I have a baby photo album you can look at."

He couldn't resist smiling. "Show me."

"A friend gave me the album at my baby shower, and I was diligent about adding pictures all through the girls' first year. Then I got lax." She pushed away from the counter. "Be right back."

Darn it. He'd grown accustomed to her standing so close. He tried not to let his disappointment show, but a long exhalation escaped.

"In here," she called a minute later from the living room. By the time he joined her, she was lowering herself onto the center couch cushion, a thick pink photo album in her hands. Patting the empty place to her right, she said, "Sit."

He did, liking this much better than standing together in the kitchen. There, legs and shoulders and elbows weren't touching. He swore a mild electric current traveled between them. Some things never changed.

She laid the album across her lap and opened it. On the inside cover was a comical white stork wearing a delivery hat and holding a smiling baby swaddled in a blanket. All the shower guests had signed the front page, adding cute little sayings and well wishes.

The next pages displayed a series of swirling black-and-gray photos. "These are my ultrasounds. You can see the twins. There." She traced an image with her fingertip, eyes bright with what must be cherished memories.

Spence didn't tell her that he really couldn't discern much of anything in the photos. He'd hate for that lovely light to dim.

"I have a DVD, too," she added, "if you want to watch that. It's of my ultrasound at about five months.

He couldn't imagine what was on it, but said, "Sure."

She laughed softly, perhaps aware he was indulging her.

The next page revealed pictures of infant Paige and Sienna taken in the hospital. Their red, wrinkled, funny-looking faces were surrounded by a bright pink background.

"Newborn pictures are never the best," Frankie explained.

Spence needed a moment. Swallowing, he waited for his heart to sink back into place from where it had lodged in his throat. These were his daughters when they were just a day, maybe hours, old! How tiny they must have been. And delicate. Yet so very perfect.

"I think they're beautiful."

"I might have extra copies stored in a drawer I can give you, along with the thumb drives."

He nodded, not trusting himself to speak.

The rest of the pictures were every bit as amazing and wonderful and adorable. The girls sleeping side by side in their bassinets. Lying atop a blanket in a sunny spot on the floor. Nestled together in Frankie's lap. Crying while their beaming grandfather held them. Happily waving their arms in the air as they sat in some kind of baby seat.

"I wish I'd been there," Spence said without thinking, and realized with a start how much he really did wish it.

Frankie turned her face to his, and tears shone in her eyes. "This is harder than I thought it would be."

"Aw, honey. Don't cry."

She didn't scold him for calling her by his favorite endearment. Encouraged, Spence put an arm around her.

They sat like that for a minute or two. She shifted, and he considered removing his arm before she did it for him. Instead, she angled her body toward him and lifted her chin.

What the...? He gazed down at her, momentarily confused. This was something she'd done when they were dating and wanted him to kiss her.

Wait. Take a breath. Think.

He had to be mistaken, right? Kiss her? When she'd very clearly set boundaries? The next instant, she raised her mouth, his whispered name on her lips as she lightly pressed them to his. Spence didn't move at first. Then he did.

Not all old habits were bad. He and Frankie slipped into this one with such ease, they might have never stopped. And it felt good. Right. Natural.

Spence suppressed a groan. He'd always loved their hot, hungry kisses. But the truth was these soft, tender, sweet ones totally undid him, reaching places inside him no one had before and probably never would.

Sure, he still wanted to whisk her off to bed. He was a guy, after all, with a healthy sex drive. His reasons, however, stemmed from his heart rather than satisfying any physical need.

His hands traveled a familiar path, raising to cradle her cheeks and tilting her head to the perfect angle. With minimal coaxing from him, her lips parted, and the first taste of her nearly sent him over the edge. He held himself in check, though how long he'd last was questionable.

Suddenly, the photo album shifted on her lap, a subtle reminder their timing wasn't the best. If not for that, Spence would have gone on kissing Frankie all night and into the next morning.

"That was…" He needed air. A dousing with cold water. Something to clear his head.

"Yeah," she agreed, her gaze roaming his face. "It was."

He smiled, hoping that was what she wanted to see. Apparently not, for she wordlessly closed the photo album and set it on the coffee table.

"Mommy, I'm thirsty."

Hearing Sienna's small voice, Spence froze. Frankie, on the other hand, was already halfway to her feet.

FRANKIE FOLLOWED SIENNA into the kitchen, her heart pounding like the bass drum in a marching band.

It's okay. Don't panic. She didn't see anything.
Sienna's unconcerned behavior set off no

alarms. Nonetheless, Frankie cringed. How could she have been so stupid?

Back when she and Spence were dating and couldn't keep their hands off each other, getting carried away was a regular occurrence. But in those days, she hadn't been a mother with two children in the house. In the next room!

"Just a few sips, okay? You know you can't drink too much before bed."

She handed Sienna a cup of water while checking the stove clock. Eight thirty? Already?

Spence appeared in the doorway, filling it with his broad-shouldered frame. "Can I help?"

"We're good," Frankie said, her sense of control returning. "I'm going to get the girls ready for bed. I won't be long."

He stepped aside. "Good night, angel face." The smile he gave Sienna was filled with affection, as was the tone of his voice. "Tell your sister I'll see her later."

Sienna practically glowed, and Frankie's resistance wavered. She'd robbed Spence and her daughters of these precious moments for years.

Robbed herself, too. Not to mention Spence's parents. In all fairness, she couldn't let it continue.

"Come on, Mommy." Sienna tugged on Frankie's hand.

There might never be an ideal time to tell the girls about Spence, regardless of how long they waited. And given the chance, she'd procrastinate indefinitely, as previously proved. Perhaps they should just do it.

She met Spence's gaze, searched his eyes and felt her conviction grow. "Would you like to help tuck them in? Tell them a story?" She inclined her head. At his arched brows, she nodded and mouthed, "Yes."

"Um, okay. Yeah."

"Let me get them changed into their pajamas and their teeth brushed." That would give them both time to pull their thoughts together.

"Sure. Sure." He shifted and tugged on his shirt collar.

Seeing him struggle for composure somehow boosted Frankie's confidence. "Don't worry.

We'll all be fine. I promise," she said, and believed it.

There were bound to be a few difficult questions to answer. Hurt feelings and confusion. Perhaps some tears. Eventually, this night would be a memory. If she and Spence handled themselves well, the memory would be a cherished one.

"Let's go, sweetie." She shepherded Sienna down the hall and to the girls' bedroom.

Having an established bedtime routine didn't stop the twins from dragging their feet. There was always some excuse to delay the inevitable. Not wanting to wear the same pajamas a second night in a row. One of the dogs chewed a favorite hair tie. The red shirt or blue shorts or pink socks weren't clean for preschool tomorrow and nothing else would do.

Finally, the girls were ready and sitting on their beds, faces scrubbed and teeth brushed. Frankie's prior reservations started to return, which shouldn't have surprised her. She had been going back and forth since the day she'd taken the home pregnancy test.

"Read Dr. Seuss." Paige requested another of their bedtime rituals.

Would Spence understand her indecision and agree to wait? Not likely, and not when he was readying himself even now.

Frankie bolstered her courage. "Tonight, we're going to do something different." She went around the room, collecting toys and putting them away. "I—we," she corrected herself, "are going to tell you a story. A true story. Wait here." Padding to the end of the hall, she peeked around the corner and beckoned Spence. He stood in the living room, staring at the pictures on the wall and restlessly tapping one booted foot. "We're ready."

He turned quickly, as if a shot had been fired, then visibly attempted to shake off his nerves. When he approached, she reached out and, taking his hand, squeezed his fingers. Rather than let go, she continued holding his hand as they walked down the hall to the girls' room.

At the doorway, they paused. Paige and Sienna stared, uncertainty on their faces.

Frankie produced a bright smile and entered, Spence behind her.

He looked slowly around the room, taking in the matching twin beds, covered by Disney Princess spreads, which in turn were covered by stuffed animals and dolls. On the wall above the side-by-side dressers, Dr. Seuss characters pranced and frolicked among printed sayings like "One fish, two fish," and "From there to here, and here to there."

Taking the chair from the corner, which usually just collected discarded clothes, Frankie moved it to the center of the room and indicated for Spence to sit. She then settled next to Paige and motioned for Sienna to join them. With a child nestled on each side of her, she began, conscious of every word she uttered.

"I need both of you to listen carefully, okay?"

Paige and Sienna exchanged cautious glances before directing them at Spence. He fidgeted, but only slightly.

"We will," Paige spoke for both her and her sister.

"Earlier today, Mommy told you that Spence and I went to school together and have known each other a long time. Well, there's a lot more we didn't tell you. Spence is someone very special to me." Frankie reminded herself to breathe. Here was the first hard part. "He was my boyfriend. You know what that is, right?"

"You liked him," Paige said.

Naturally, her more precocious daughter caught on. Cara's stepson, Nathan, attended the same preschool as the girls. Paige had taken a shine to him some months ago. That was until he scribbled all over her backpack with a marker and made her cry.

"I did like him." Frankie sent Spence a small smile. "I still do." She didn't want the girls detecting any discomfort between them.

"I like your mother, too," he added. "Very much."

Paige and Sienna listened intently, though

confusion continued to cloud their features. Frankie needed to get to the point soon.

"Four years ago, Spence left. For a job. In California." Not entirely accurate. He'd drifted before hiring on at Cottonwood Farms. But that was superfluous information best saved for another day. "After he left, I found out I was going to have a baby. Two babies."

Frankie paused, purposely slowing down her racing thoughts. This was a defining moment in their lives. Everything would be different from now on. She absolutely needed to say the right thing.

Spence rose from the chair, startling her. As she blinked in astonishment, he went over to Sienna's bed and sat down directly across from them. He was so close, his knees bumped Frankie's.

Leaning forward, he regarded each girl, his expression serious, yet reassuring. "What your mom's trying to tell you is I'm your dad."

At Spence's declaration, Paige sat up straight.

Sienna gasped softly and clutched a plush elephant to her chest.

"I had no idea until the other day. But now that I know, I couldn't be happier." A wide grin spread across his face. "You both are everything I've ever wanted in a daughter. Pretty and smart and absolutely adorable."

Paige and Sienna twisted to gape at Frankie, eyes wide and mouths open.

"Mommy…?"

She drew them close, hugging their small bodies. All in all, Spence was doing a good job. Better than she'd expected. Ultimately, however, she believed the girls would take their cue from her. If she projected uncertainty or anxiety, they would become uncertain or anxious.

"I'm happy too," she said brightly. "I've been hoping your daddy would come home."

"And I'm here to stay," he added.

Wait. Were those tears in his eyes? She'd seen Spence get emotional only once before, that last time when she'd told him they were through, and she didn't want to see him again.

"Don't worry." His voice broke. "We're going to take our time getting to know each other."

"Yes, we are," Frankie agreed. "No rush."

"Why did you go?" Sienna asked Spence.

Here it was. One of those difficult questions.

"I had a job." He wisely stuck to the basics. "Your mom didn't want me to go. We had a big fight. But if we'd known she was having you two, nothing would have made me leave."

Frankie waited, hoping they didn't ask why she'd kept her pregnancy a secret.

"Will you live with us?"

Whew. Paige's question was much easier to answer. "No, sweetie, he's not."

"Why?"

"Well…" Okay, maybe not that easy.

Spence cut in, once again impressing her. "Your mom and I haven't seen each other for four years. We decided I should stay at my own place for now."

His explanation was probably more than Paige and Sienna understood. Even so, they seemed satisfied.

Spence went on to tell them about their other grandparents, aunt and uncle and cousins, which the girls found very exciting.

"Can we see them?" Paige beamed.

"Of course."

"When?"

"Soon. They'll be happy, too."

Though the hardest part was past them, more difficult questions were bound to arise. Possibly for years to come as the girls matured. Frankie thought about checking with the administrator of the local support groups that met at the church in town. Maybe the woman could recommend a counselor to help guide and advise them.

Feeling the effects of the last hour like a heavy weight on her shoulders, Frankie patted the girls' knees. "Mr. Sandman's been waiting long enough, and we have an early morning."

Of course they protested, with claims of not being tired.

"I'll see you tomorrow." Spence stood and fondly caressed each twin's cheek. "Good night."

They remained a little reserved. Frankie assumed that was normal under the circumstance.

"I won't be long," she said, as he left the room.

Rather than kiss the girls and shut off the light, she stayed and sang them a song. Before long, their eyelids started to droop.

"Can we sleep with you if we get scared?" Sienna turned on her side and snuggled her stuffed elephant in her arms.

"Yes." Frankie tucked each girl in. "But there's nothing to be scared of."

Paige rubbed her eyes and murmured, "Do we call him Daddy?"

Frankie had anticipated this question. "Only if you want to."

A minute later, she tiptoed away, leaving the door slightly ajar. She found Spence standing at the kitchen counter, drinking coffee from a mug.

"I hope you don't mind," he said. "I helped myself to some instant decaf."

"Not at all."

He lifted his mug. "Want some? You look like you could use a boost."

She shook her head. "I am tired, though."

"Too tired to talk?"

"Can we wait until tomorrow? I have the first shift at the café."

"I'd like to start paying child support. Right away."

Apparently, he hadn't heard her. "I'm not going to refuse you. We just need to agree on how much."

"I did some asking around. Called a couple divorced buddies." He named a monthly sum. "That's about average."

It was more than average. Frankie had done her own checking, off and on in recent years. "That's too much." She named an amount she considered fair.

"I can afford more."

"You're starting a horse farm and will need money. Besides, you've already given me ten thousand dollars for my catering business." Something she still didn't feel quite right about.

"That's different."

She pushed her hair back from her face. "Really, I'm exhausted. Mentally and physically. Can we please postpone this until tomorrow?"

"You're right. I'm sorry. I just can't believe how well Paige and Sienna took the news."

Frankie supposed he wasn't being intentionally naive. Just brand-new to parenting. "They're still processing. I fully expect them to struggle and have more questions. Possibly require some counseling."

"They'll be fine. You worry too much."

His tone struck her as dismissive and rubbed her the wrong way. Crossing her arms over her middle, she said, "I don't want you to hurt the girls. They're young. And emotionally fragile."

"Why would I hurt them?"

"Maybe not intentionally."

"Not for any reason."

"When you're a parent, your children come first. Every decision you make must take them into consideration."

"I get it." A small furrow creased his brow. "Like I told you and them, I'm staying."

"Forgive me for being frank, but I've heard that before, and yet you left."

She could practically see his hackles rise. Well, too bad. She would protect Paige and Sienna at all costs. Even at the expense of her relationship with Spence.

"Guess I was wrong," he said. "Things didn't go that well tonight."

"They did. But Paige and Sienna could still have problems adjusting."

"Young children adapt quickly."

"And you know this because you have so much experience at parenting?"

He gave a dry, humorless chuckle. "You haven't changed one bit."

Frankie instantly stiffened. "What does that mean?"

"You still don't want me involved in our daughters' lives."

"That's not true."

"No? You're pushing me away. At the very

least, making damn sure I know the boundaries."

"You're being unfair."

"Am I?" Setting down the mug, he squeezed past her and went to the living room.

Huffing, she spun, annoyed that he'd forced her into going after him. He'd grabbed his cowboy hat off the coffee table and was heading for the door.

"Spence."

"You're tired, Frankie. You said so yourself." He turned the knob. "We'll talk tomorrow."

"Fine. I'll call you."

That seemed to amuse him, for he gave another dry chuckle before leaving.

Frankie half stormed, half walked to her bedroom, deciding to shower away the tension coursing through her. She wasn't wrong. The girls needed more than one little talking to, no matter how well it went, in order to adjust. Hadn't Sienna asked if they could sleep with Frankie? Deep down, they were grappling with insecurities.

Spence never looked beyond the immediate present. That recklessness and impulsiveness, she supposed, was a part of his charm. It was also a huge contributor to their past problems and, clearly, their current ones. Shame on her for not learning her lesson.

Chapter Eight

"No. I'll do it." Spence stepped in front of Mel Hartman and prevented her from lifting the mare's right front hoof.

She braced her hands on her hips and forced an unconvincing scowl. "I'm a veterinarian. Specializing in large animals."

"You're pregnant. I'm not taking any chances."

He was confident neither of his former racing mares would kick or bite. He'd securely confined this one in the wash rack, restricting her mobility. But accidents happened, and he would never forgive himself if Mel was injured. Then there was Frankie. She'd refuse to ever speak to him again.

"You tell me what you want," he instructed Mel, "and I'll do the heavy lifting."

"I'll be fine," she insisted.

He didn't budge.

When he'd sat with Frankie's sisters in the booth at the café the other day, he hadn't noticed Mel's slightly protruding stomach behind the tabletop. Now, he regretted calling her. Because she refused to leave and insisted on completing the exams, he was monitoring her every move—and would willingly take a kick to his most sensitive places in order to spare her.

She narrowed her gaze. "You know, I'm going to have to get close to feel for the foal."

"Maybe we should tranquilize her."

"I'm not giving her any unnecessary drugs."

"Do you have an associate I can call instead?"

"Spence." Her annoyance promptly evaporated, and she started to laugh. "All right. We'll do things your way." She indicated the mare's hoof. "Let's take a look. I noticed she favored that foot when you brought her out from the stall. She might have an abscess or contracted a case of thrush during the long trailer ride."

When nothing appeared amiss with the hoof, Mel finally convinced Spence to let her near enough to run her hand down the mare's leg and also feel her underside. But only from behind the wash rack railing, and with him standing right there.

Fortunately, and predictably, nothing happened short of the mare cranking her head around to inspect Mel's hair.

"She's a beauty, Spence." Mel evaluated the mare from head to tail. "And the foal appears fine. Good size and moving around."

"Should we have an ultrasound done?"

"I honestly don't believe it's necessary. She shows no visible signs that the pregnancy is in distress. Of course, if you really want one, I'll come back tomorrow with the machine. But in my opinion, you're wasting your money."

"What about her limp?"

Mel tapped a finger on her chin, considering. "I don't see cause for concern. Maybe she simply pulled a muscle during the long drive. I suggest you take her on some easy walks for the next few days and see how she is after that. Call me if there's no improvement."

Spence's other mare passed her exam with high marks—and only a few grumbles from Mel, when Spence intervened. Relieved, he returned the mare to the stables and then met up with Mel at her truck.

She already had an invoice prepared and handed it to him.

Spence read the total. "You didn't charge me enough."

"I gave you the family discount."

"But I'm not family."

"You're my nieces' father."

He might have been more than that. Like her brother-in-law, for instance. But after last night, and the way he and Frankie had left things, he wasn't sure anymore.

"Thanks." After pulling his wallet from his

rear jeans pocket, he withdrew enough bills to cover the invoice.

Mel must have read something in his expression, for she said, "Frankie mentioned you told the girls last night that you're their father."

"Yeah. We did." Was their conversation casual or had Frankie complained about Spence to her sister? "I think it went well."

"She said the girls had more questions this morning at breakfast, but nothing she couldn't answer."

"What kind of questions?"

Spence propped an elbow on the hood of Mel's truck. They'd always gotten along in a younger-sister-of-his-girlfriend way, and he respected her opinion. Hadn't she warned him that last time not to leave, saying Frankie wouldn't be happy and might break up with him? He'd chosen not to listen, convinced he could sweet-talk Frankie as usual.

"Mostly about your family." Mel finished stowing her medical supplies while they chatted. "According to Frankie, Paige and Sienna are fascinated with their new relatives. They asked when they were seeing you again."

"Really?" That was better than he'd hoped. "I want to see them again, too." Today, if possible.

Mel looked at him with interest. "You're happy about being a dad."

"I am. I admit, it took me a day to get used to the idea."

"That kind of news is a shock when you're not expecting it." She patted her belly. "Aaron needed time to process after my big announcement."

"The girls are growing on me. Fast."

"Have you told your folks yet?"

"I'm calling them after you leave." He'd texted his mom this morning, asking when she and his dad would both be available.

"Oh, good. They'll be thrilled."

Still convinced she'd undercharged him, Spence watched Mel pull away. He debated phoning or texting Frankie about coming by later in the day. His mother was bound to ask for pictures of the girls, and he'd forgotten to take any yesterday. Plus he wanted to give Frankie his child support payment.

Right. Who was he kidding? Certainly not himself. He wanted to talk to Frankie about their argument last night.

After considerable thought, he'd decided he might have been too quick assuming that, because the girls reacted well initially, they'd easily adapt, moving forward. On the other hand, he wasn't wrong about Frankie's attempts to, if not keep him at arm's length, then resist his involvement.

Granted, he'd made some mistakes in the past. Let her down. Disappointed her. But no matter how valid she'd believed her reasons were, she'd been seven kinds of wrong not to tell him about the girls. All those lost years he could never get back.

Removing his phone from his shirt pocket, he noted he'd missed a text from Cara Dempsey reminding him of the adoption event committee meeting tomorrow. Typing as he walked, he sent her a return message confirming he'd be there for at least part of the meeting.

He might have regretted volunteering if not for Cara's enthusiasm and his support of what he considered a worthy cause.

Finding a secluded bench behind the stables, where he could sit in the shade and talk to his parents in relative privacy, he leaned back, stretched out his legs and dialed their number.

"Spence, sweetie!" His mother's cheery voice greeted him after the second ring.

"Hi, Mom. How you doing?"

"Your dad's bursitis flared up. He's resting on the couch. I just put a fresh ice pack on his shoulder and gave him some more ibuprofen. He refuses to see the doctor, of course." They chatted briefly, until Spence asked her to find his dad and put the phone on speaker so they could both hear him.

A minute later, his dad's booming voice filled Spence's ear. "Your mares arrive yet?"

"They did. Yesterday." Before his dad could

ramble on, Spence said, "I have some news for you and Mom. Big news."

"You and Frankie are back together!" his mom blurted in an excited voice. She'd always adored Frankie and was devastated over their breakup.

"No. But it does involve Frankie."

"Oh?"

"I'm not sure how to say this, so I'll just come out with it. Are you both sitting down? If not, grab a chair."

"Just tell us, son," his dad insisted, "before your mother has a stroke."

"Frankie has twin daughters. They're almost four."

Complete silence followed for several seconds.

"Spence?" His mom's voice shook. "What are you saying?"

He swallowed, fighting a sudden tightness in his chest. He hadn't realized how affected he'd be, telling them.

"Their names are Paige and Sienna. And I'm their father."

"What? My God. You can't be serious." His mother started babbling something to his father.

"Mom. Calm down. I can't understand you."

"How is this possible? Why didn't she tell you?"

"It's a long story. She didn't find out she was pregnant until after I left."

His dad cleared his throat. "I hate to say it, but are you sure these girls are yours? I tend to think most women would hunt down the man who got them pregnant."

"That's a part of the long story."

His mom interrupted him. "You can tell us later. I want to hear about Paige and Sienna." She spoke the girls' names with something like reverence.

For the next fifteen minutes, Spence recounted meeting the twins for the first time, and their day yesterday. As expected, his mother insisted on hearing every detail. Twice, she stifled a soft sob.

"I'm hoping to see them again tonight," he said, and promised to send pictures.

His father, who'd been mostly quiet, cleared his throat again. "Have you thought about getting an attorney?"

"Frankie and I have agreed on child support payments."

"Look, son. You sound happy and your mother's beside herself with joy. But you really should obtain legal advice. Frankie did hide your children from you for years. It's a little suspicious, if you ask me."

"Do you have to bring that up now?" his mom demanded.

Spence could imagine her glaring at his dad and possibly punching him lightly on his unaffected arm. "It's okay, Mom. Dad's right. I'd be stupid not to consult an attorney."

Frankie could change her mind. Last night was a good example.

"I'm sure Warren can recommend someone," his dad said, referring to the friend and attorney who handled his parents' personal matters.

"I'd appreciate that." Spence stood and brushed dirt from his jeans, left there from the old bench. "Look, I hate to cut this short, but I have an appointment to look at a rental house."

Sooner or later, he was going to have to find more permanent digs than Eddie's spare room.

"Call us tonight."

"Yes, Mom." He knew better than to refuse. "Love you guys."

He'd barely hung up when his phone chimed. Frankie's number appearing on the screen started his pulse racing.

Placing the phone to his ear, he said, "I was going to call you later."

"Hi," she began tentatively. "I was wondering, are you busy tonight?"

"Not at all."

"Any chance you could come over?"

"Absolutely." Apparently she wasn't that put out with him.

"I got a call. A big catering job. Fifty pounds of brisket for a VIP luncheon tomorrow."

"Whoa. Kind of last minute, isn't it?"

"They're willing to pay extra. I need..." She paused again. "Help. Sam and Ronnie left earlier for the rodeo, and Mel's busy. Seeing as you're my business partner, I—"

Spence didn't let her finish. "I'll be there. What time?"

"I'm heading to Scottsdale as soon as I'm off work. There's a wholesale supplier with quality product on Thomas Road. I prefer buying my meat from them. The girls can go with me. They've been before. Can you meet us at the house around seven?"

"No problem."

"And bring whatever personal stuff you need. Smoking brisket is a twelve to fourteen hour job. You'll be staying all night."

Don't look! Don't you dare.

Frankie forced her gaze away from her phone, refusing to check the time. Spence had said he'd show by seven. Sooner or later, she had to start trusting him. A little at least. About things like punctuality.

She disliked the renewed friction between them and was baffled at his inability to see reason. The girls absolutely had to come first. If he charmed them, like he'd always charmed her, then took off again as was his habit, they'd be devastated. Their relationship, so new and tentative, would end up in shambles. If that happened, Frankie would never forgive him.

"The heck with it," she grumbled, and snatched her phone off the patio table. Tapping the screen, she activated the display. It showed 7:06 p.m. He was late again. "Figures."

Setting the phone back down, she checked the temperature on her two smokers, added the meat and shut the doors with a satisfied nod. Before long, rising smoke would drift away on the mild breeze. Her neighbors were always stopping Frankie to comment on the delicious aromas coming from her backyard whenever she and the girls were out walking the dogs.

Don't look.

Naturally, she did. Why hadn't Spence answered her text? Knowing she'd be outside and unable to hear the doorbell, she'd told him to come though the side gate. Should she call?

An angry squeal had her turning toward the grassy area where the girls played with the dogs. Correction, *had* been playing with the dogs. Bozo and Miss Muffet now sat in front of the French doors, pleading to go inside and escape the mayhem.

Sienna squealed again, the result of Paige throwing a handful of sand at her. Last year, Frankie's dad had built the sandbox for the girls as a birthday gift. They loved it. Frankie, not so much. She was tired of cleaning sand out of shoes and clothes and mouths and, yes, hair.

Slinging the dish towel she'd been using as a hot pad over her shoulder, she marched across the yard. Thank goodness she'd gotten both smokers going before this latest interruption. "Paige! What have I told you about throwing sand?"

She stared up at Frankie with unabashed innocence. "It was an accident, Mommy."

Right. Just like last week.

"Stay put." She leveled a finger at Paige. "Don't move." Pivoting, she reached for Sienna.

"You're all right, sweetheart. It's only sand and will wash out."

Sienna burst into sobs. Frankie brushed as much sand as she could from her sensitive twin's hair and clothes. Using the end of the dish towel, she wiped her face and mouth.

"Mommy, don't." Sienna pushed Frankie's hand away.

Rather than reprimand her, Frankie ceased her efforts. Sienna was too young to realize she wasn't mad at Frankie but rather her sister.

"He's here!" Paige hollered, just as the dogs raised the alarm. "Our daddy."

Our daddy? Not quite the same as "Daddy," but close. Perhaps they were easing into it.

Spence closed the gate behind him and, waving hello, crossed the yard, a bulging gym bag at his side. Hmm. While Frankie had told him to bring what he needed, she'd meant a toothbrush and a clean shirt for tomorrow. He appeared to have packed an entire change of clothes, a pair of shoes, and possibly pajamas. Did he need pajamas to sleep on the couch?

"Hiya, angel face." He stopped and gave Paige a brief hug.

She beamed. Then again, she was the twin who loved attention.

Sienna's sobs instantly ceased, and she slowly approached Spence, determined to be included.

"What happened to you?" Instead of hugging her, which was a smart move, as Sienna often shied from physical contact, he lowered his face to her level. "You've been crying."

"Paige threw sand at me," she murmured.

"It was an accident." Paige feigned contrition.

"Did you apologize?" Spence asked.

"Um…"

"She didn't." Sienna glared at her sister.

"Do you think you should?" He raised his eyebrows.

"I'm sorry." Paige kicked at the ground with the toe of her sneaker.

"I brought you something." Spence set down his gym bag and unzipped it.

Frankie inched closer. Was he trying to buy

their daughters' affection? The idea didn't sit well with her.

Reaching into the bag, he withdrew two coloring books and held them out to the girls. "One has puppies, one has kittens."

Sienna squealed again, only with delight. For once, she beat her sister to the punch and grabbed the kitten coloring book. Luckily, Paige was equally delighted with the puppy one.

Spence's hand went into the bag again. "I figured you already have crayons, but I brought a box, anyway."

Frankie might have been amused or charmed if she wasn't busy having reservations. More than once when they were dating, he'd added a token gift to his winning smile when sweet-talking her out of being mad. Kind of like when he'd brought ice cream.

"Mommy, look!" Paige whirled and held up her gift. "A coloring book."

"I see. What do you say?"

"Thank you," both girls chorused.

Spence grinned. "You're very welcome."

"Come on, Sienna!" Paige grabbed her sister's arm.

"Don't run off just yet." Spence plucked his phone from his shirt pocket. "I want to take some pictures for your grandparents."

"I haven't had a chance to make those copies," Frankie said. "Sorry."

"No worries. You've had a busy day. And from the looks of it—" he nodded at the smokers "—a busy night ahead."

"Yeah."

Spence patted the girls' heads, as naturally as if he'd been doing it all their lives. "Let's go over there. The light's better."

Paige and Sienna skipped after him, Paige chatting up a storm.

They were adapting quickly, Frankie mused. That, or Spence was a yet-to-wear-off novelty.

"Take one with Bozo and Miss Muffet," Paige gleefully suggested.

The dogs tolerated exactly three pictures before Frankie granted their fervent wish to go inside.

Paige had an idea for another picture. "Mommy, take one of us with our daddy."

Frankie swallowed, her conflicting emotions refusing to play nice with each other.

"Do you mind?" Spence handed her the phone, then knelt down, a girl on each side.

They didn't cling to him, or he to them, but their smiles were big and bright. Frankie positioned the phone, a lump forming in her throat. Had things gone differently, taking pictures of Spence and the girls might have been a common occurrence. She didn't say anything when no one suggested she be in any of the shots, telling herself she was making a big deal out of nothing.

Spence sat at the table and scrolled through the pictures, the girls looking over his shoulder and offering their opinions. Together, they chose several of the best ones, which Spence then e-mailed to his mother. Next, he pulled up pictures of his parents and brother's family to show the girls.

"Maybe this weekend you can talk to them."

Paige nodded enthusiastically, Sienna hesitantly.

"Have you ever video chatted?"

"What's that?" Paige asked.

While he attempted to explain, with some of what he said going over the twins' heads, Frankie checked the smokers. Part of her was glad the girls were accepting Spence and excited about meeting his family. The other part of her worried about how quickly Spence was becoming a part of their lives.

She'd allowed it. Heck, in some ways, she'd encouraged it. Like kissing him last night on the couch, for example, and requesting his help tonight. What if by letting him in, she was setting herself and their daughters up for heartache? His track record didn't inspire confidence.

"Hurry up, you two," she abruptly said, inexplicably annoyed. "Bath time."

The protests were loud and emphatic. The girls desperately wanted to stay up.

"I'll be here in the morning," Spence promised. "We can have breakfast together."

"Pancakes," Paige exclaimed, with Sienna quickly seconding her.

"Anything I can take care of for you?" he asked Frankie.

She sent the girls inside before showing him how to refresh the wood chips. "Add more in another thirty minutes if I'm not back by then."

"Got it."

Wood chips. Not difficult. Surely he could handle that small task without messing up.

Bathing and the remainder of their nighttime routine took forty-five minutes. When Frankie finally returned, it was to discover Spence had changed into basketball shorts and a sweatshirt.

She paused at the doorway leading outside, her heart skipping erratically. She'd seen him in casual clothes a thousand times. Just not in her backyard. Something about it felt...intimate.

"You hungry?" she asked, rather than join him outside. Five minutes. That was all she needed to shore up her defenses.

"I ate earlier. But left room for dessert." His

innocent expression was exactly like the one the girls affected when attempting to sway her.

"There's some blueberry cobbler in the fridge and leftover ice cream from the other night."

"Oh, honey. You're killing me."

His tone, warm and sexy and so very familiar, affected her the way it used to by seeping past the defenses she'd carefully erected. Damn him.

"Be right back. Watch the wood chips." She quickly retreated before doing something stupid like, she didn't know, flirting maybe.

Chapter Nine

Frankie procrastinated, taking a full ten minutes to warm the blueberry cobbler and add ice cream. The brisket would be fine. Corralling her emotions, not succumbing to Spence's charms, those things were more important. Paige and Sienna needed a mother whose control wasn't obliterated by a sexy grin.

With a renewed sense of determination, Frankie went outside to the patio, plate in hand. When Spence saw her, he broke into an enormous grin, the kind moments earlier she'd warned herself to resist.

He's just happy about the blueberry cobbler. That's all.

Then explain why his gaze never left her face and seemed to center on her mouth.

"I forgot to give this to you earlier." He shoved a hand into his sweatpants pocket and produced a check.

She set the cobbler on the table in front of him. "You don't have to pay me for food."

"It's child support. For the rest of this month and next month, too."

She accepted the check and sat, noting the amount was what they'd agreed on, no more and no less. Good. He was starting out on the right foot. "Thank you."

Dropping into his chair, he attacked the cobbler. Between bites, he said, "I contacted an attorney today. He's drawing up a preliminary custody agreement and will send it to your attorney, if that's okay." He downed another large spoonful. "Unless you've already done one."

"No, not yet."

Nothing like talking about attorneys and custody agreements to squash any romantic mood. Not that her mood had been elevated. Mostly, it was bouncing all over the place.

"He was recommended to me by my folks' attorney." Spence paused, spoon in midair. "I told them today. About the girls."

"I figured as much when you took pictures. What was their reaction?"

"Mom's thrilled and can't wait to meet them."

Only his mom? What about his dad? Frankie silently scolded herself. She was needlessly overanalyzing.

"Mom wants to visit this weekend," he added, "but they're having a big sale at the dealership. Would Tuesday or Wednesday be okay?"

"I work both those days."

His features fell. Frankie's guilt soared.

"But I'm sure I can switch days with Shelly Anne."

Asking to introduce his parents to their granddaughters was a reasonable request, especially when the Bohanans were willing to drive the seventy miles from Marana. The least Frankie could do was accommodate them.

"I'll fix us a nice lunch," she offered. "Something casual. I think it would be best for Paige and Sienna if they met your parents here in familiar surroundings."

He startled her by reaching across the table for her hand. A tingling sensation traveled up her arm, warming her skin from the inside and triggering silent alarms in her head.

"This means a lot to me.

"I'm, um…" Angry at herself for once again falling under Spence's spell, Frankie reclaimed her hand. "Of course. I've always liked your parents."

"They've always liked you, too."

She made sure to place her hands in her lap, well away from danger. "When's the last time you added fresh chips?"

"Twenty minutes ago."

"Ah. Okay."

Spence promptly finished his cobbler and

wiped his face with the napkin she'd brought. "What's the game plan for tonight?"

Glad to change the subject, Frankie explained the ins and outs of monitoring the smokers all night. "Stop adding fresh chips after midnight. Then it's a matter of making sure the smokers don't shut off for any reason. So, no sleeping on your shift."

"Do they tend to shut off?"

"I lost power one night in June," Frankie said, "and it wasn't restored until morning. If that were to happen tonight, there's no way I could deliver the brisket on time."

"Which is why you have a portable generator."

So, he'd noticed. "Dad gave it to me." She stood, and together they walked over to where the old but reliable generator sat up against the house. "There's enough gas for six hours. Don't hesitate firing it up. I don't care about the noise."

After showing him how to start the generator, she took his plate and spoon into the kitchen. Because he'd changed into more comfortable clothes, she did the same thing, donning fleece

leggings and a T-shirt and throwing an old
shawl over her shoulders before going outside.

Not a single thing about her outfit screamed
sexy, yet the flash of desire in his eyes was undeniable. Not wanting to encourage him, she
asked, "First or second shift?"

"I don't care either way."

"Then I'll take second shift." Barring any
problems, she'd be able to squeeze in a short nap
after delivering the brisket and before going in
to work. "I'll set up my tablet for you. Stream-
ing movies helps pass the time."

"If you need to get to work tomorrow," Spence
said, "I can deliver the brisket. I have some errands to run, anyway. And I told Cara I'd stop
by the planning meeting for the adoption event."

"Thanks, but I like to personally meet the
customers."

This job was simply too important to her
fledgling business not to warrant her full attention. She wasn't sure how much longer she
could continue working at the café; the envi-
ronment had changed since Tia Maria's nephew

took over. And Frankie wasn't the only employee contemplating her future.

Wait a minute. Who was she kidding? She would work there as long as necessary, even if she hated it. Frankie wasn't ready to give up her benefits and couldn't afford the monthly health insurance premiums on her own.

Had Spence covered that in the custody agreement? She'd know soon enough, when her attorney received the draft.

"Who's watching the girls?" Spence asked, scattering her thoughts.

"They can come with me to deliver the brisket."

"What about while you're at work?"

Frankie had made a couple calls, hoping to find a substitute babysitter to take her sister Sam's place. So far, she'd had no luck. "I'm thinking of calling one of the other preschool moms in the morning."

"I can watch them."

"You've done so much already." Truthfully, Frankie wasn't ready for such a big step.

"I'll take them with me to the committee meeting. Cara mentioned her kids will be there."

Frankie hedged. "Maybe I could call work and get the day off."

The twinkle in his eyes dimmed. "I'm not a complete incompetent."

She bit her lip, unsure how to take his remark. Had she hurt him? And if so, what if he went from being cooperative to stubborn, insisting he had rights and making her life difficult?

"Is asking you to check in with me every hour too overprotective?"

He nodded. "Easy enough."

Knowing she'd be a wreck the entire time, she agreed, anyway. "All right."

He abruptly got up and added fresh chips. Frankie noted the time; he'd remembered while she'd forgotten. She wasn't reassured. There was a big difference between monitoring smokers and supervising two active little girls.

She also noted the rigid set of his shoulders. That was her fault, she supposed, and her responsibility to fix.

"I got a call earlier today on a used commer-cial smoker," she said. "The seller originally wanted more money, but now he's lowered his price."

"Is it in good shape?"

"I've only seen pictures. I told him I'd drive over on my next day off."

"Want me to go with you?"

Technically, Spence was one of her inves-tors and had a right to an opinion on major purchases. And it was his contribution to her crowd-funding campaign she'd be using to buy the smoker. Still, she resisted. This was her business. She was the one in charge.

Before she had a chance to answer, Spence jumped back from the smoker, wringing his hand and swearing softly.

"What's wrong?" She rushed toward him. "Are you okay?"

"It's nothing." He shoved the side of his hand into his mouth.

"You're hurt."

He chuckled. "Those smokers get pretty hot."

"Let me see."

"I'm fine."

She sent him a disapproving look, the same one she used on the twins. He reluctantly presented his hand for her inspection. She took it in hers and moved them to a spot beneath the light in order to examine the burn.

"In my professional opinion, you'll live," she pronounced. "An ice pack will soothe the sting."

"I already feel better. Must be the mom touch."

"Paige and Sienna usually require a kiss before they quit fussing."

"A kiss?" His voice lowered. "Even better."

Shoot! Frankie had spoken without thinking. Leave it to Spence to derive a totally different meaning from her words.

"Well, y-yes," she stammered. "But they're little."

Spence dipped his head. "I'm a kid at heart."

She backed up, averting her face. He was not kissing her again. Not tonight. Things between them were getting way too cozy as it was.

"I'll get my tablet."

His hand must not hurt much, for he placed it on her arm. "That can wait."

"It's late. I should go to bed soon."

"Frankie." He tugged gently.

"No," she stated firmly, and established ten inches of much needed space between them. "I can't. I won't."

"Did I do something wrong?" If he was wounded by her rejection, he did a good job disguising it with annoyance.

Wait a minute. Why was he mad? He had no right to any expectations simply because they'd kissed twice in the past two days, and almost a third time.

All right, all right. Granted, she was running hot and cold. He could be confused.

"I apologize if I've given you the wrong impression. I'm not ready to pick up where we left off. There are still too many unresolved issues. We need to concentrate on reaching an amiable custody agreement, and on developing the girls' relationship with you and your family.

"You can't deny you have feelings for me."

"Whether I do or don't is irrelevant. I won't let the girls get hurt."

"Like I said before, I care too much to let that happen."

She straightened her spine. "I've been and will continue to be accommodating as long as you continue to be a good father. I admit I may have allowed myself to…resume old habits, and again, I apologize."

"You asked me here tonight," he said.

"In order to help me with the brisket. You're the logical choice, as you own a percentage of the catering business. That was my only reason."

"You kissed me last night."

That was true—she'd initiated their kiss. "I realize now I made a mistake. We were looking at the photo album, and I became sentimental."

"All right," he said brusquely, and increased the distance between them. "You've made yourself clear."

As had he, stating from the start he'd come home to woo her.

"Fine. I'll be right back."

"Never mind." His voice could slice steel. "I can read or watch movies on my phone."

"Good night, then."

Frankie wanted to kick herself. She shouldn't have let him near her, shouldn't have let him kiss her, if she wasn't prepared for the consequences. The fact she had trouble resisting him or had wanted to satisfy her curiosity weren't good enough reasons.

SPENCE FINISHED CHANGING clothes in the hall bathroom, using liquid soap from a butterfly dispenser, a pink washcloth and matching towel to freshen up. Somewhere around four o'clock, he'd finally drifted off, only to waken at six thirty when his phone went off.

He'd jackknifed to a sitting position, took two seconds to remember he was on Frankie's couch and then grabbed his phone off the coffee table where he'd left it. Had any name other than his friend Lucas Palmeroy's appeared on the display, Spence would have let the call go to voice mail. But Lucas didn't typically phone unless it was important.

By the time Spence finished his conversation, Frankie had come in from the patio, looking every bit as weary as he felt. They'd exchanged a few polite words about the brisket, which was nearly done. Neither of them mentioned their argument the previous night before he'd disappeared into the bathroom.Examining his stubbled jaw in the medicine cabinet mirror, he debated shaving with the disposable razor he'd brought. Outside the door, Paige's and Sienna's high-pitched voices came and went. By the time he emerged, marginally revived, the twins were sitting at the breakfast bar, hair adorably mussed, swinging their fuzzy slipper–covered feet.

"Good morning," he said, mustering as much energy as he could.

"Mommy's making pancakes," Paige announced.

Indeed, Frankie stood at the stove, a spatula

in her hand. "There's a glass of orange juice for you already poured."

Sienna pushed the glass toward him, gifting him with a shy smile.

"We're helping Mommy with the brisket." Paige's pronunciation of brisket sounded more like biscuit.

Spence lowered himself onto the empty third bar stool and took his juice. "Did she tell you I'm watching you this afternoon while she's at work?"

Both girls' mouths dropped open, and they gasped with delight. At least, he hoped it was delight and not terror.

Frankie turned from the stove. "I haven't yet." A mild reprimand laced her voice.

At the moment, Spence didn't care. She'd agreed, and he intended to make sure she kept her promise.

"We're going to The Small Change Ranch, where the mustang sanctuary is."

"To see some horses?" Paige exclaimed.

"I wish, but I have a meeting. Some other kids are supposed to be there."

"Nathan from school and his little sister Kimberly," Frankie told the girls.

"Eww." Paige wrinkled her nose.

"What's wrong?" Spence drained his orange juice.

"I don't like him. He colored on my backpack."

"That's Nathan?" The boy from her preschool. The one she'd liked until he'd committed the unforgivable. How could Spence have forgotten? "You can play with his sister."

"She's a *baby.*"

"Babies can't play?"

Spence looked to Frankie for assistance and got absolutely none. Shrugging with a kids-will-be-kids attitude, she dropped pancakes onto plates.

Slow start aside, breakfast went well. Spence offered to wash the dishes while Frankie got the girls dressed and the food containers ready for transporting the brisket. He finished first and knew he should hit the road. Lucas was waiting for him. Except he stayed, killing time by repacking his gym bag and checking e-mails on his phone. Finally, Frankie emerged from the girls' bedroom.

"I have an appointment in Florence," he said. "I'll be back before noon."

"What?" She stopped to frown at him. "That's an hour drive each way. It's almost eight now. I have to be at work in four hours."

"That gives me plenty of time."

"Why didn't you tell me this last night?"

"Because Lucas didn't call me until this morning."

She huffed with obvious annoyance. "I'll find someone else to babysit."

"No, Frankie."

"We talked last night about you putting the girls first."

"This appointment's important and directly relates to my ability to provide for the girls. Lucas has a young colt he'd possibly like me to train. I need a job—I don't want to live off my savings. He's willing to pay me a salary plus a percentage of the colt's winnings."

"In Florence? Are you planning on moving?"

Spence held his temper. She was overreacting. "My only plan is to look at the colt and talk to Lucas. But, for the sake of argument, if I accept the job, commuting is an option. Lots of people drive an hour each way to and from work. There are also closer places where the colt could be stabled and trained. Nothing's been decided."

"Won't you have to go on the road when this colt races?"

"Yes. But if he wins, I'll have the chance to earn good money, of which a portion will go toward the girls. Might be enough so you can quit the café and build your catering business."

"And if he doesn't win?"

"I'd still be paid my salary."

"You just returned, and now it feels like you're leaving again."

"I'm not leaving, Frankie. I'm simply exploring an opportunity. I have kids to support now, and horse trainer jobs don't grow on trees. I may need to cast a larger net, one that extends beyond Mustang Valley."

She relented, but she didn't look happy. "I leave for work at eleven forty. On the dot."

"I won't be late. You can count on me."

Spence departed after a quick goodbye to the twins. Frankie escorted him to the door, her "Have a safe trip" sounding more perfunctory than sincere. All in all, quite a bit different from their previous partings.

The trip to Florence passed quickly. While boasting a rich Western history and plenty of tourist attractions, the town was still mostly known for its state prison.

Frankie probably hadn't liked the idea of Spence working in Florence for just that reason. Which was ridiculous, in his opinion. Lucas's property was located on the opposite side of town, closer to the golf course and upscale housing communities. If Spence ever brought the girls to visit, they wouldn't be anywhere near the prison.

His and Lucas's meeting went well. Spence

liked the looks of the colt and was impressed with his speed and agility when the exercise rider took him for a spin on the practice track. They discussed terms over coffee. Lucas, whom Spence had met often during his years at Cottonwood Farms, was a straight shooter. He was also opinionated, and Spence worried they might disagree on training methods.

In the end, they shook hands and parted, agreeing to a two-week-long trial period to determine if Spence was a good fit, and if he and the colt took to each other.

While traffic had cooperated earlier, a freeway accident on the drive home caused a twenty-minute delay. Spence was already cutting it close, and prepared himself for another of Frankie's lectures.

All right, maybe he shouldn't have dallied over that second cup of coffee with Lucas. But, damn, he'd needed the caffeine boost after his lack of sleep.

At precisely 11:46, Spence arrived at Frankie's, pretty pleased with himself. If not for discovering an unexpected shortcut, he might have been considerably later.

She stood in front of the open garage, the girls' car seats on the ground by her, impatiently tapping her toe, her phone pressed to her ear. Glaring at him, she said something into the phone, probably telling her plan B that he'd arrived.

He shut off the truck and climbed out. By then, Paige and Sienna had wandered out from the garage. Waving as if he wasn't late and hadn't committed one or two driving violations during the last ten miles, he strode toward them.

Frankie cut him zero slack. "Clocking in late doesn't help my already strained relationship with the new manager. He made it clear when he started that there would be personnel changes. I could be fired."

"Then you'd better hurry."

The café was a ten-minute drive. She could make it by the skin of her teeth if she left right that second.

"I shouldn't have to, Spence."

"Point taken. But arguing with me won't get you there faster."

"Call me every hour," she said, repeating her number one priority.

"Yes, ma'am."

"They'll need a nap soon. No later than two or they won't sleep tonight."

"We won't stay for the whole meeting."

After giving him a spare house key, Frankie kissed each girl, admonishing them to be good. She didn't add, "For you father," not that Spence had expected it.

He held the girls' hands and stood to the side while Frankie backed out of the garage and drove—very slowly, in Spence's opinion—away.

"How about we meet your grandparents?" he asked, taking the girls inside. "Make that video call we talked about yesterday."

Sitting between them on the living room couch, Spence opened the app on his phone. Before he could place the call, the girls started fighting over who got to hold the phone first.

Spence decided to flip a coin. They were both so fascinated by the coin-tossing process, Paige didn't even mind that Sienna won.

As he'd anticipated, they were initially shy. Sienna tucked her head into Spence's side and had to be coaxed to look at the screen. Paige's exclaiming, "I can see myself," finally did the trick.

He smoothed the way as best he could with introductions.

"You are both so beautiful." Spence's mom wiped her damp eyes with a tissue when she talked, and didn't appear to mind that neither girl held the phone steady.

Even Spence's normally stoic dad was emotional and needed to clear his throat several times. "I can't wait to meet you on Wednesday."

With their anniversary sale in full swing, Spence's parents reluctantly ended the call after thirty minutes.

"I promise to bring you a surprise when we see you," his mom said.

"What kind of surprise?" Paige asked eagerly.

"If I told you, it wouldn't be a surprise." She blew a kiss, which the girls returned.

Spence sat still for a moment, absorbing the enormity of what had just happened. He'd introduced his parents to his daughters. That was huge. Life-altering. He breathed deeply, feeling a tightness in his chest.

"Do you have Teddy Bear Playground on your phone?"

Paige's questions worked like a loud gong, breaking into his thoughts. "What's that?"

"A game, silly."

"I don't play games on my phone." He pressed a fingertip to her nose.

The twins' disappointment couldn't have been greater. Sienna covered her face with her hands, while Paige threw herself back onto the couch cushion and groaned in agony. Spence was determined not to fail this first big test.

"Can we download it?" He opened the store app on his phone and clicked the search bar.

Once the game was installed, the twins

showed Spence how to play. Sad to say, he didn't catch on right away.

"Teddy Bear Playground is harder than it looks," he proclaimed after his third loss.

When he laughed good-naturedly, both Paige and Sienna grabbed his arms, pretending to pull him in different directions. Not exactly a hug, but close, and enough to cause his heart to swell with love. The kind of love that would only grow stronger and more powerful with each day.

How could Frankie worry for one second that he'd leave Mustang Valley? Even if he had to go on the road with Lucas's colt or any one of his own, he wouldn't be gone long and would always return.

"Hey, be careful," he teased. "I'll break in half." Their uproarious giggles said they didn't believe him. Unable to let that pass, he tickled each of the twins' necks before getting up. "Anyone hungry?"

"Yes!" Paige popped off the couch.

Sienna did, too. "We want ramen noodles."

Great. Something Spence actually knew how to prepare, and that didn't take long.

With the girls' help, he found the noodle packages in the pantry and a pan in the lower cupboard. A search of the refrigerator yielded the addition of carrot sticks, string cheese and milk to round out the meal. After lunch, they headed out for his meeting at The Small Change.

Something quite baffling happened to the girls between the time they left the house and arrived at the ranch house. Spence had no clue what triggered their one-hundred-eighty-degree mood swing, but suddenly, they were whiney and irritable and fussing.

He lifted Sienna out first. The very next second, his phone went off. Frankie's name appeared on the display.

"Hi. We're fine," he said. "Just got to The Small Change."

"You didn't call."

He held the phone out to check the time while opening the passenger door on his truck. "It's ten after one."

"You're supposed to call every hour."

"Sorry. Didn't realize it was supposed to be *on* the hour."

Paige suddenly screamed, evidently mad at Sienna for some reason.

"What's wrong?" Frankie demanded.

"Nothing." Spence unbuckled Paige's seat belt. "Just a minor disagreement."

He handed the phone to Sienna so that she could chat with her mother while he helped Paige out. As soon as he had, she ran around the truck and grabbed the phone away from her sister despite Spence's warning to wait her turn.

"I wanna talk to Mommy."

In the mild fracas that ensued, Spence's phone was dropped. He reached for it just as the girls burst into tears.

"I don't know what happened," he said to Frankie. "They were getting along fine, and the next second, they weren't."

"They're tired. They should nap."

"We won't stay long. Once the committee's firmed up the details on the race, we'll leave."

"That's probably for the best." She offered no other words of wisdom.

Spence walked the girls to the front door, flipping a coin to see who got to ring the bell. His trick didn't work as well as the last time. And once inside, things only got worse.

Chapter Ten

Frankie entered the house through the garage door. Juggling her purse and a half-dozen to-go boxes from the café, she navigated the laundry room and the short hallway leading to the kitchen.

"Hey. Where is everyone?"

"Mommy!"

Paige burst into the kitchen, Sienna a heartbeat behind her. Frankie dumped her purse and the boxes on the counter a microsecond before being bombarded. Miss Muffet circled them and barked with excitement, while Bozo wagged his tail and panted.

Accepting a hug and kiss from each girl, Frankie straightened. "Where's, um, your dad?"

At that moment, Spence stumbled from the direction of the bedroom. Frankie stared, blinked and then stared more.

"What happened to you?"

"Things got a little hectic. But not out of control. I should warn you, though, the house is kind of a mess."

He ran a hand over his disheveled hair. Several stubborn tufts refused to lie flat. One side of his cowboy shirt had come untucked, and there was a stain down the front, possibly fruit juice. Or blood? He appeared frazzled, disconcerted and winded, as though he'd run a marathon through a complicated maze.

"Welcome to parenthood," she said.

"I'll do better next time."

"I'm not sure you did bad." She started opening the food containers. "Everyone's alive and in one piece."

"You're being kind."

Her first inclination had been to read him the riot act. That way, he'd try harder in the future. Except then she'd looked at him and remembered how difficult it had been for her in the beginning, taking care of two babies. Some days, most days, she still struggled with balancing her children, her job, her family, her home, her catering side business and her personal life, which received the least attention.

"Let's eat." She handed each twin a box. "Set these on the table." Plates and flatware came next. "Sit down, everyone."

"I should get going," Spence said.

"Stay. There's plenty of food."

"You sure?" He eyed the table hungrily.

"Miss lunch today?"

"I guess I did. The girls had ramen noodles, and snacks at the ranch."

"Happens a lot. Forgetting to eat, that is."

The dinner, fried chicken with all the fixings, was consumed with gusto. Frankie was treated to a complete account of the afternoon, from

Paige and Sienna. Spence needed all his energy to simply shovel food into his mouth.

"Nathan pulled Sienna's hair," Paige reported, properly indignant. "And Kimberly stole my cookie on purpose."

"Then she threw up on Paige." Sienna squealed with laughter. "She had to wear one of Nathan's shirts."

"How humiliating." When Spence stopped halfway through his meal, Frankie told him, "Eat. You need to keep up your strength."

He bit into a chicken leg.

"What time did they nap?"

"Don't be mad. Three thirty. But not for long. The doorbell rang and woke them. Someone running for the school board. I left the flyer on the coffee table."

"We talked to our nana and papa," Paige announced.

"My parents," Spence clarified. "A video call."

"They have a surprise for us."

That topic lasted until the end of dinner. Any

other night, Frankie would have insisted the girls take a bath. Instead, she gave them permission to play in their room while she and Spence cleaned up. When she checked on them a short while later, they were both fast asleep on top of their bedcovers.

Not bothering with pajamas, Frankie slipped off their shoes and socks and put them to bed. One night without bathing or brushing their teeth wouldn't ruin them for life.

"Everything all right?" Spence asked when she returned.

"Fine. They were both sleeping. Guess you tuckered them out."

"I can say the same about myself."

"I don't suppose you're interested in a cup of coffee."

One side of his mouth tilted in a smile. "Well, since you're twisting my arm."

Rather than hand him a mug, she carried both to the living room, where they could be more comfortable. Sitting with him evoked memories from their kiss the other night, and Frankie was careful to hug her side of the couch.

"Thanks. This hits the spot." He took a sip, his expression thoughtful. "I owe you an apology."

"For what?"

"There's a lot more to being a parent than I thought. Makes me realize just what an incredible job you've done with Paige and Sienna."

"I appreciate that." She blew on her coffee. "And while we're in the mood, I apologize, too. I was rough on you today. Unnecessarily so. And a nag."

"I am new at this."

"But you're a natural. Like I always suspected you'd be."

"I have a lot to learn."

"You do," she agreed, "and you will. There's more to good parenting than being entertaining and winning your daughters' affection."

"Like disciplining them and setting rules?"

"You saw for yourself today how trying it can be when the girls squabble and misbehave. Just wait until you're up all night tending a sick, crying child who refuses to be consoled. That's a real test of patience."

"Like I said, my admiration for you continues to grow." He sat back, absently kneading the back of his neck as if it ached.

In the past, Frankie would have offered a massage. Not tonight.

"I was wrong about something else," she admitted. "I did lead you on. Gave you reason to have expectations. Then, yesterday, I abruptly changed gears."

"Yeah, well, I see now we need to take a break. Figure things out first. I downplayed the girls' ability to adapt to change because I wanted them to immediately accept me as their dad and for us all to be one big happy family."

She nodded. And though there was more they could—and probably should—discuss, she changed the subject. "How did the meeting go? Kimberly throwing up on Paige notwithstanding."

"Good. I say that because Cara seems happy.

They've picked two horses to race against Prince, and she's lined up some good prizes."

"Like what?"

"Let's see." Spence went from kneading his neck to scratching his head. "Gift cards. A day at some spa. Free tune-up from Conroy's Auto Repair. Dinner at the café. Passes to the state fair. I can't remember the entire list."

"Are you using Sam for one of the jockeys?"

"We are. The adoption event's one week from today. That doesn't give the committee a lot of time to advertise the mock race and solicit donations. Cara thinks a young gal riding a local celebrity horse will be a huge draw."

Frankie supposed she understood Cara's reasoning. She just wished Sam wasn't so young. "Won't the other jockeys have an advantage? They've got much more experience than Sam."

"But they won't have had the chance to practice on their horses before the race like she will."

"Anything else interesting happen today?"

"Like my trip to Florence?"

Frankie had been curious all afternoon but

hadn't asked during her four phone calls. Wait, make that five.

"Lucas offered me the job," Spence said.

"Huh." She mulled that over for a few seconds, debating the pros and cons.

"I didn't say yes." He waited a beat. "I didn't say no, either."

"You're thinking it over," Frankie guessed.

"We agreed to a two-week trial period. If the job's not for me, or I'm not right for the job, I move on. No hard feelings."

"That sounds actually…" She pretended to draw back with dismay. "Who are you and what did you do with Spence? He always jumps in both feet first and wearing a blindfold."

"I told you. I've changed."

For her, the jury was still out. But he'd definitely made strides. Four years ago, Spence would have taken the job with no trial period, then up and quit without notice if he didn't like it.

"I have some news. Good news." She smiled.

"The client today was really happy with the brisket."

"That's great."

"Actually, it gets better. She referred me to a friend of hers. The friend called on my way home from work. They're having a gigantic family reunion two weeks from today. Over three hundred people. They want an estimate for brisket, ribs and chicken."

"Three hundred people? You're kidding! Can you manage that much food?"

"Yes, with a commercial smoker. I called that guy from Craigslist back and left a message."

"My offer to help still stands." Spence smiled appealingly.

"What about your job?"

"I'm free evenings."

"Then I accept." She was going to need his help if she had any hope of transporting the smoker home and catering the reunion.

He must have read her mind, for he asked, "What about labor? You can't do everything alone."

"If Sam's busy with a rodeo, I'll recruit Mel and my stepmom. Her foot will be better by then."

"If we have to hire someone, I'll cover the cost."

"No, you won't."

"Frankie."

"Let's just see what happens." She set her coffee down and started to rise. "Speaking of which, I owe you for last night."

He reached for her arm, tugging her back down onto the couch. "Reinvest the money in the company."

"That's not the agreement we have per the crowd-funding terms."

"Then use it for the girls."

"You already gave me child support."

"I helped you last night as a favor."

"No." She twisted to face him. "I'm going to pay you, you're going to accept the money and we aren't going to fight about this anymore."

"New rules?"

"Look, we're partners. As parents and in business. Rules aren't bad. They keep our expectations and responsibilities clear. I agree we've slipped a few times, but not again."

"You're sure about that?" His tone was teasing. He no doubt also recalled the last time they'd sat on this couch.

"We both have a lot on our plates. And two daughters who need our undivided attention during a crucial time. Let's not make a mistake by rekindling an old romance that's bound to end disastrously."

"*Disastrously* is a strong word."

"Spence," she chided.

"Right." He blew out a resigned breath. "You win."

"This isn't a competition."

"Of course not."

They talked for a while about nothing of consequence. And while Frankie should have been glad they'd cleared the air, she missed their former easygoing exchanges.

Here was the trade-off, she supposed. No one got what they wanted without losing in return.

Funny, she'd been wondering lately how different their lives would be if she'd told him about the twins from the beginning. Now she wondered how different their lives would be if she and Spence had truly gotten over each other, moved on and weren't still wildly attracted to each other.

SPENCE HAD ATTENDED plenty of horse auctions in his life. The event put on by the mustang sanctuary was much the same. A mobile auctioneer's booth had been set up at one end of the ring. Spectators occupied bleachers. Two helpers assisted the auctioneer, spotting bidders and interacting with the crowd. Horses were brought in, usually one at a time, and after demonstrating their abilities, sold to the highest bidder.

There were several differences, however. All the horses there today were formerly wild mustangs. Every individual helping was an unpaid volunteer, and proceeds, down to the last dime, went to support the nonprofit sanctuary instead of being split between the sellers and the auction company.

"That is one ugly dude." Esteban Rojas elbowed Spence in the ribs while making a face. His heavily accented English wasn't always easy to understand. To compensate, he often expressed himself with big gestures, which were in stark contrast to his diminutive stature.

Andy Drummand agreed. "What rock did they find him under?"

He stood next to Esteban, the difference in their heights no more than an inch. They'd arrived that morning, flying in from California, and would return tomorrow afternoon. Spence was making sure they were well treated during their stay. He'd been lucky to find two competent jockeys free this weekend and willing to make the trip.

Pushing his cowboy hat back for a better look, he examined the "ugly dude" in question. Stocky and shaggy, the mud-brown gelding did indeed possess a prominent Roman nose, along with small ears and a stubby forelock that more closely resembled a Mohawk.

He was being led around the ring by a teen-aged girl and carrying Cara's stepson, Nathan on his back as proof of his calm disposition. The gimmick obviously worked, as the horse sold for a decent price to a family with three children after an intense bidding war. Cara beamed, as she did with each and every banging of the auctioneer's gavel, pleased another horse had found a good home.

Before long, Spence and his jockey buddies would drive to the makeshift track behind the pastures where the mock race was being held. Sam, too, whenever she arrived. Prince and the two mustangs pitted against him were waiting in the stables, a team of volunteers grooming every inch of them to perfection and braiding their manes and tails with colorful ribbons.

Because Esteban and Andy didn't have to pre-pare like they would in a real race, they were enjoying the adoption event, having their pictures snapped with excited fans and giving interviews for the local TV station.

Spence, on the other hand, watched people mob the betting counter—in reality a folding table manned by more volunteers—and tried to shake off his nerves. The mock race was the highlight of the adoption event and the reason for the record-breaking crowd. Cara was counting on a sizable amount of money being raised.

No reason for him to feel pressured.

Right.

Fortunately, ticket sales were through the roof and the fishbowls in front of the donated prizes filled to overflowing. The flat-screen TV donated by Spence's parents' dealership was one of the most popular items.

Frankie had donated a complete meal, courtesy of I-Hart-Catering, the official name of her business as of this week. She'd had flyers printed up, and she and the girls were handing them out from their station near the betting counter. Spence had been keeping one eye on them since the event started.

"Ha! Look at your *niñas*." Esteban gave Spence another rib jab.

Paige and Sienna had somehow gotten hold of a young pigmy goat, probably belonging to a friend of Frankie's. The goat wore a turquoise harness and leash much like a dog's, and a kerchief around its neck.

It willingly followed the girls like a puppy. Hopping, twisting, bleating and generally acting pretty cute, it attracted people with kids, and many without. Anyone coming near was immediately handed a flyer. Frankie, it seemed, was capitalizing on the opportunity.

Esteban and Andy had been amazed to learn Spence was a father. When introduced, they'd charmed the girls and been respectful to Frankie. Then teased Spence about how pretty Frankie was and that he was a fool to let her get away.

Spence didn't bother explaining the complexities of his and Frankie's relationship. Hell, he hardly understood them himself.

This past week, he'd seen her and the girls

daily, for longer and shorter amounts of time, depending on Frankie's schedule. He'd abided by her request to keep things friendly but platonic. It was hard, though not impossible. He just had to make sure they weren't alone together and that they didn't touch, accidentally or otherwise.

"Jeez, Bohanan." Andy gave his head a dismal shake. "You have it bad for her."

Spence returned his attention to the ring. "What are you talking about?"

"Your girlfriend. You can't stop staring at her."

Esteban laid a hand over his heart and batted his eyes. *"Es amor verdadero."*

Spence didn't have to speak Spanish to understand the meaning. "She's not my girlfriend, and we're not in love," he said.

"Buddy, you can't fool us." Andy smiled smugly.

So much for hiding his feelings. Spence said nothing. Any reply he made would only be more fodder for his friends' jokes.

"Let's load up the truck and check the equipment."

The jockeys reluctantly pushed themselves off the fence and accompanied Spence. He sneaked one last look at Frankie and the twins, Esteban's voice playing in his head.

Es amor verdadero.

They hadn't gone far when a familiar white-haired figure in a bright yellow jacket, and using a walking cane, crossed their path. Spence smiled as recognition dawned.

"Annily Farrington. What are you doing here?"

"I came to see you." Her wrinkled face lit up as she opened her arms for a hug.

"Me?" Spence squeezed hard before releasing the well-liked friend and associate from his days at Cottonwood Farms.

"When I heard you were racing mustangs, I figured I had to see for myself."

She turned to greet Esteban and Andy, who'd both heard of her and expressed delight in finally having the chance to meet her. The racing world was a small one. Annily Farrington was one of the better known owners of racing quarter horses, having made a name for herself over the last four decades.

"You came all the way from Fort Worth?" Spence asked.

She dismissed him with a wave. "Not even a gander of your handsome face would get me to travel that far. I came from Rio Verde."

The next town over? "What are you doing there?"

"I bought a small ranch. Downsized my operation and moved last month. Doctor's orders. I have to slow down. Problem is I'm not yet ready to quit the business. Kept my best horses."

She didn't offer the nature of her health problems, and Spence didn't ask. "We're practically neighbors," he said instead.

"My feelings will be hurt if you don't come for a visit real soon."

"Name the day."

"Call me." She reached in her pocket and withdrew a business card.

"Can I bring my twin daughters? They're three, almost four."

"Love to have 'em. Got a couple of my own grandkids. Miss 'm something awful. My daughter moved her family to Florida first of the year."

"I thought she was going to take over from you one day."

Annily gave a sad sigh. "That was more my dream than hers, I'm afraid. She met a man. He's the reason she moved." Annily sighed again. "I briefly considered finding a new business partner, then decided I'd try downsizing first. I've never been the easiest person to get along with. Hate to put that burden on someone I like."

"You?" Spence laughed. "You're the definition of amenable."

"Comes from being right all the time," she quipped.

He hated leaving her, but the auction was wrapping up, and the race would start soon.

They said their goodbyes and promised to meet up after the race.

Seeing such a good friend raised Spence's spirits, and he whistled a tune as he, Esteban and Andy meticulously attended the saddling and bridling of the racing mustangs before loading them into the trailer for transport to the makeshift track. Spence had inspected the track the previous day with Frankie's dad, Ray, and hadn't left until he was satisfied with its condition.

He'd been half expecting a lecture from Ray for leaving his daughter to raise the twins alone. That hadn't happened, and to Spence's surprise, the two of them got along as well as they always had in the past.

Esteban and Andy headed off to the office to change into their "racing silks"—neon-colored polo shirts and tan breeches. In a real race, their uniform would represent the owner and farms for which they rode.

While Spence had his head stuck inside the truck cab, Sam arrived. She was also wearing her "silks" and a pair of high black boots. In one hand, she carried a riding helmet.

"You look ready," Spence said, taking her in.

"I'm nervous."

"You'll do great."

She'd been practicing the last few days and working hard. Spence thought if she ever wanted to switch careers from barrel racer to horse racing, she might make a decent exercise rider, and possibly a jockey.

The next moment, Esteban and Andy emerged from the ranch office. Spying Sam, they came over, and the three of them engaged in conversation. Esteban and Andy were enjoying mentoring the young woman, and she basked in the attention.

"You all look fantastic! I love your outfits."

Spence spun at the sound of Frankie's voice. Paige and Sienna skipped ahead of her, flyers clasped in their hands.

"Hey, you—" At the last second, he added, "three," in order that Frankie wouldn't think he had eyes for only her.

"We're helping Mommy." Paige proceeded to drop all her flyers.

She and her sister wore matching jeans and sweatshirts, one of several gifts from his mother. The introduction Wednesday had gone well, with Frankie pulling out all the stops and putting on a delicious lunch. Though hesitant at first, Paige and Sienna had eventually warmed to his mother's patient coaxing.

They were still in awe of his father, who boomed even when using his inside voice. He'd taken their reluctance in stride, confident they would get used to him.

The funny thing was his father, along with the gray beard he sported, were what the twins talked about the most. They'd asked Spence a half-dozen times already when they were seeing "Papa" and "Nana" again.

Spence stooped and picked up the flyers for Paige, smoothing her hair as he straightened. "Here you go, angel face."

"What about me?" Sienna asked.

He tugged on her ear. "You, too, sweetie."

They threw their arms around his legs, alternately shouting, "My daddy," and "No, *my* daddy."

He swayed momentarily, unbalanced as much from the twins' antics as from the fact that his heart was on the verge of exploding.

Frankie caught him by the arm. Heat from her fingers instantly seeped into his skin. Their gazes locked. Held.

This was the closest they'd been in over a week. He almost said, "I've missed you." Almost.

Behind him, Esteban muttered something in Spanish. Spence was pretty sure the jockey had called him lovesick and poked fun at his sappy expression. Spence slowly extracted his arm from Frankie's grasp. He swore he felt their disconnection like a physical tearing apart.

"I know the race starts soon," Frankie said. "We won't keep you."

"I've always got time for my girls."

Her eyes widened ever so slightly. She didn't ask if she was one of his girls, and he didn't say.

"I finally negotiated a deal on that smoker."

That got his interest. "The seller come down to your price?"

"Close enough." She grinned, obviously happy with herself. "He also has a used chest freezer for sale. It would be nice to have one if business picks up. That way, I could buy meat when it's on sale and be able to store it."

"How much does he want for the freezer?"

"You're not giving me any more money, Spence. Don't even—"

"What if I bought the chest freezer and just let you borrow it?"

She groaned with exasperation.

"Let me at least pick up the smoker for you."

"That'd be great." She peeled the girls off him. "We should get going. Dad promised to save us a good seat for the race."

Spence bent and opened his arms. "Give me a hug, kiddos, and wish me luck."

They squealed when he squeezed hard. All Frankie gave him was a wave over her shoulder while walking away. He nodded in return.

If she wanted to act as if something hadn't just passed between them, well, he could, too.

Not that he'd had much of a choice. Like it or not, Frankie was calling the shots. For now.

Chapter Eleven

With everything ready at the starting line, and assurances from Ethan Powell that he would wait on the signal, Spence hopped a ride in the back of Ray Hartman's pickup to the finish line.

When he arrived, the local TV news reporter was interviewing Cara Dempsey. She did an admirable job plugging the mustang sanctuary and the plight of wild horses not just in Arizona but all over the western United States.

After they were done, Spence approached the

attractive young woman and her camera opera-
tor. "Can I ask you folks a favor?"

She flashed a megawatt smile that had unde-
niably helped her career along. "What's that?"

"You mind filming the finish? I can't imagine
the race will be neck and neck, but just in case
the winner's in question, might be a good idea."

"Perfect. We were going to ask you if we
could film the race."

Spence showed them the best place to stand.
"You should also have a good shot of them coming down the track."

Ultimately, Spence had decided on a three-
quarter-mile, straight-line track. The mustangs,
while fast, weren't racehorses, and a shorter
track was probably best for their health and
safety.

Seeing the crowd grow, he phoned Ethan for
an update. Spectators had started lining up
on the west side of the track, down the entire
length. Ranch hands and volunteers were managing the crowd, keeping them far enough away

to avoid distracting the horses and potentially causing an accident.

The trailer they'd used was parked a hundred or so yards from the starting line and separated the jockeys and their mounts from the crowd. At the designated time, they'd walk the horses to the starting line, somewhat like at a real race, then climb on and wait for the flag to drop.

"Theo McGraw's going to call the start of the race," Ethan said. "We located a bullhorn for him to use, and a flag."

Spence strained to hear above the noise. "That's great!"

He had the utmost respect for the owner of The Small Change Ranch and knew of no one better for the important job of official starter. Not only was the older gentleman a respected lifelong member of the community, he'd donated the use of his ranch for the auction event and the race, as well as cleared and graded the back road for the makeshift track.

"I think we should delay the start," Ethan said. "People are still coming."

"Okay. How are the horses and jockeys holding up?"

"They're fine. Just a regular day for them."

As Spence had expected. These mustangs weren't high-strung Thoroughbreds. They weren't even excitable racing quarter horses.

"Check back with me in ten or fifteen minutes," he said.

Disconnecting from Ethan, he turned and found himself face-to-face with Frankie's dad.

"How are *you* holding up?" Ray asked.

"Not bad."

He clapped Spence on the back. "I imagine you're busier than a hound dog in flea season, but can you spare a couple minutes for me?"

"What's on your mind?"

Ray began walking, and Spence fell into step beside him, his curiosity piqued.

"I've supported the sanctuary since it was first started," Ray said. "It's nice to see you taking an interest. Means a lot to folks here in town."

"Glad to help."

"I've been wanting to tell you how happy it

makes me that you finally got the chance to be a father to those beautiful girls. When Frankie made it clear she wasn't going to tell you, and said none of us should go behind her back, well, I didn't agree with her. But she's my daughter, so I respected her wishes."

"I understand, sir." Here was that talk Spence had been expecting yesterday.

"I'm not the kind to butt in, and don't want you taking what I'm about to say as interfering."

"Guess that will depend."

They stopped where the dirt road turned, far enough away not to be heard by anyone, while close enough for Spence to keep an eye on things.

"You've done right by Frankie these past few weeks," Ray continued. "You could've made it hard on her. Taken her to court. Punished her for being unfair to you. And maybe she deserves it."

"I'm not like that." Spence wasn't offended. He remembered Ray as someone who spoke plainly.

"Mighty glad you aren't. Because the girls are the ones who would've suffered the most if you had."

"I agree."

"Are you planning on staying, then?"

"That's what I've been saying all along."

Ray hitched his chin at the gathering crowd. Frankie's blue minivan had arrived and parked while they were talking. She opened the rear driver's side door, revealing Paige and Sienna.

"Those two little girls are falling for you," Ray said. "Please don't hurt them."

"That's the last thing I want."

"Or Frankie. I don't think she could survive a second time."

Did no one have faith in him? How much, Spence wondered, did he have to do, how hard did he have to work, to prove himself? To earn their trust?

His phone rang, and he answered it without looking. "Yeah."

Ethan's voice filled his ear. "I think we're almost ready."

Spence watched Frankie take the twins' hands and glance around. When she spotted him and her dad, she waved.

"Give me five minutes. I'll call you." Spence repocketed his phone. "Going to have to ask you to excuse me, Ray."

"'Course. Good luck with the race. Pretty exciting."

Spence went right to Frankie and the girls. "What are you doing here?"

"We're watching the race," Paige announced.

Not to be outdone, Sienna said, "We gave away all Mommy's flyers."

"That's great."

"Is it all right?" Frankie looked at him expectantly. "That we're here? I asked Ethan. He said he didn't mind."

Spence leveled a finger at all three of them. "You have to stay out of the way. I'm serious. And no running off. We practiced a few times with the horses. That's no guarantee they won't act up or run off the track."

"We will." Frankie didn't move. "I thought

you should know the race has raised almost four thousand dollars. Your friend Annily Farrington donated five hundred. She didn't even want any tickets."

"She's a good person."

"All this—" Frankie gestured "—what you've accomplished, it's special, Spence. I'm really proud of you."

Proud? She'd never said that to him before. Certainly not with such sincerity.

"Thanks."

"We're also here because we…" She shrugged. "Because I would like to be at the finish line with you."

"Why?"

Her admission had to contain a deeper meaning. His question certainly did.

The answer to both would have to wait, because his phone rang again.

"Everyone's getting impatient," Ethan said.

"Hold on." Spence took Frankie's elbow and gave her a small nudge. "Get behind the line. All of you."

They obliged, hurrying to catch up with Frankie's dad. He lifted first one twin and then the other into the bed of his truck for a better view.

Spence spoke to Ethan. "We're ready at this end."

A minute later, Spence heard the distant sound of Theo's voice blaring from the bullhorn. "And they're off!"

He clicked his stopwatch. Ethan should be doing the same.

The thundering of hooves came an instant later and was immediately drowned out by the cheers of the crowd. Dust rose from beneath the horses, giving the appearance of a small cloud moving at rapid speed. As they and the riders neared, the ground started to vibrate beneath Spence's boots.

Behind him, Frankie and the twins shouted, "Go, Sam, go."

The teenager and Prince were indeed in the lead. Spence watched them through his binoculars. Esteban and the gelding he rode were a close second. Andy and the mare were already one length behind, not any real competition.

Spence suspected Esteban was holding back, giving the teenager a once-in-a-lifetime thrill. Not that Prince wasn't the fastest horse competing, but the experienced jockey could probably win this race on a Shetland pony.

The cheers reached fever pitch as the horses closed in on the finish line. Spence was proved correct when, at the last second, Esteban and the gelding pulled forward and crossed the line in front of Sam and Prince.

Some of the cheers died, probably fans of Prince and friends of Sam. Those who'd bet on Esteban and the gelding whooped and hollered, and the crowd shifted as people began drifting off. All three riders had slowed their horses to an easy lope and were now turning them around, letting them catch their breath.

"Good job, everyone," Spence said as they walked up to him. "Congratulations, Esteban."

"I almost won." Sam's face glowed with excitement, and she couldn't sit still in the saddle.

Were she not a novice, she might have encouraged that last extra burst of speed from Prince and possibly placed first. Esteban could have let her win, but he was too much of a competitor. Spence understood.

Volunteer handlers came over to help the riders dismount and hold the horses while pictures were taken and interviews filmed. Sam was a natural: cute, bubbly and with the right amount of girl-next-door appeal.

Hearing a child crying, Spence looked over to see Paige having what appeared to be a meltdown. Even Grandpa Ray couldn't seem to console her.

Spence joined them. "What's wrong, angel face?"

"Sam didn't win."

"She did, kind of."

Paige stopped crying and lifted tear-filled eyes to him. "No."

He knelt on the ground in front of her and Sienna. "Sam made a lot of money for the mustang sanctuary. That's kind of like winning.

And she gets to be on TV. That's like winning, too. You can watch her tonight. She'll be on the nine o'clock news." He glanced up at Frankie. "If your mom will let you stay up that late."

"Only if you behave," she warned.

"We will," Sienna promised.

"Will you watch with us?" Paige asked.

"Um…" Spence rose. "I—"

"Please," Frankie said, bestowing an incredibly warm smile on him. "Come for dinner. About eight, if that's not too late. I told Dad we'd help clean up after the event, and we won't get home for a couple more hours."

"I accept." He grinned in return. "And I have things to do, too."

"Come on, girls." She started to leave, and then hesitated.

"You forget something?"

"I did."

To his shock, she returned and threw her arms around his neck. There was nothing sexual about the hug, just a friendly show of appreciation.

That didn't stop Spence from enjoying the sensation of her lovely curves pressed against him. Neither did it stop the surge of desire exploding inside him. She smelled incredible. Felt wonderful. And when she touched—

"See you tonight." Frankie abruptly withdrew, shattering the fantasy he'd been enjoying far too much.

"Yeah. Tonight." He swallowed, his throat having gone dry.

The next two hours dragged. Spence had trouble concentrating, his mind constantly returning to their hug earlier and dinner later tonight. Cara approached him while he was checking on his mares to give him the final tally. In addition to adopting out twenty-seven mustangs and two burros, the event, including the race and raffle, had brought in almost eight thousand dollars.

"Is that good?" he asked. This being his first time, he had no idea what was typical.

"Our best event yet. The goal has always been to adopt out as many horses as possible. Any additional money is a bonus. Thanks, Spence. Say you'll volunteer next year. If you're still in town."

"You can count on me."

A commitment one full year in advance? That wasn't something Spence did. Used to do, he corrected himself. Things were different now.

Finally, he was able to leave the ranch. Stopping at Eddie's first for a quick shower and change of clothes, he headed to Frankie's. Only one light shone inside the house when he arrived. Maybe they were already watching TV.

He rang the bell, and Frankie answered the door, her finger pressed to her lips.

"Shh. The girls are in bed already." She stepped back to let him in. "They were just too tired and fell asleep on the way home."

He remained standing there. "What about watching Sam on the news?"

"I set the DVR to record it."

"Maybe I should go."

Everything about her softened, from her eyes

to her posture to her demeanor. "Is that what you want?"

"No."

"Then come in. Stay."

His gaze traveled the length of her, noting her snug sweater top and hip-hugging jeans. "The way you look and the way I feel right now, it might not be the best idea."

"What if I'm having the same idea?"

"Pardon my confusion, but you've been keeping me at arm's length for over a week."

She smiled seductively. "Arm's length is much too far, don't you think?"

He went still, forced his brain to pay strict attention. He couldn't afford to misconstrue her meaning. "I need an explanation."

"Fair enough." She evaluated him in return. "I've been resisting you since the day I saw you in the café. And you've been breaking down my defenses one by one. Not with your talk, not with your charm, but by being exactly the kind of man, exactly the kind of father to our daughters, I've been wishing for my whole life.

I established rules, and you adhered to them. I set boundaries and you respected them. I asked for help and you gave it. You're not wearing me down, Spence. You're not coercing me. You're showing me what I've been missing. And believe me—that's a lot more effective. Now." She tilted her head appealingly. "Are you coming inside or do I have to ask twice?"

Spence stepped over the threshold and, without losing any momentum, swept Frankie up into his arms, kicked the front door shut behind him and carried her into the master bedroom.

FRANKIE LAY ON her side, staring over Spence's naked shoulder at the slit in the drapes. Moonlight peeked in and cast a silver line on the carpet. If she focused really hard, she could see one tiny star twinkling against a blanket of darkest black.

Should she wish on the star, as she'd taught the twins to do? She wanted so many things, picking just one was next to impossible.

For the girls to be happy and healthy. Except now their happiness depended in part on Spence and whether or not he continued to be a part of their lives.

For I-Hart-Catering to be a success. The upcoming family reunion could make or break her fledgling business. While the profits were currently being reinvested, her goal was to eventually withdraw a small salary for herself. Only then could she reduce her hours at the café or possibly even quit.

She snuggled closer to Spence, the heat from their contact warming her. *Please don't let this be the biggest mistake of my life.*

He stirred briefly at her touch, rolled over to face her and slung an arm over her middle, all without opening his eyes. The next moment, his steady breathing resumed. He was like that, always sleeping soundly regardless of where he was and what was on his mind.

Not Frankie. Guaranteed, she'd lie awake most of the night, alternately worrying about the fallout from their actions and remembering their exquisite lovemaking.

You let him into your bed.

She should follow that up with a *What is wrong with you, girl?* Only nothing had felt wrong from the moment he'd carried her into her bedroom until he'd utterly exhausted her.

There'd never been anyone else for her besides Spence. He was the only man she'd ever been intimate with, even during those long weeks and sometimes months he'd been gone while they were dating. Also the four years since he left.

Kissing didn't count. Not that she'd kissed very many guys. Frankie mentally added them up. Five? No, six. None of them had ever tempted her to go further. Not because they weren't good-looking or nice or hadn't treated her well. They just hadn't been Spence.

As much as she tried to fall out of love with him, she always failed. And now, after tonight, she might never be able to.

His skill at lovemaking had improved. She didn't dare contemplate how that had come about, convincing herself their insatiable longing for each other and extensive time apart were responsible.

She suppressed a moan as memories of the last two hours returned. Her body arching beneath his while his hands and mouth sought her most sensitive places. Pausing here, lingering there, giving her breasts and tummy and the inside of her thighs extra special attention.

He hadn't stopped despite her protests. Not until he'd brought her to a stunning climax. Finally, when she could stand no more, he'd entered her. Frankie had gasped, the shock reverberating throughout her body, before she'd surrendered to a rush of sensations.

Pinning her arms over her head, he'd driven into her, saying her name, telling her how beautiful she was, insisting she was his, now and always. Before long, she'd climaxed again. That time, he hadn't waited, but followed after her.

Frankie had prepared herself for regrets. That hadn't happened, however. She and Spence were too busy laughing and cuddling and sharing intimate conversation for reflection. But then he'd drifted off, and now she lay awake in bed, unable to sleep, her mind going a mile a minute.

She and Spence had made significant progress lately, it was true. Still, had they moved too fast? Sex rocketed a relationship ahead to a whole new level. What if he asked to move in with her and the girls? Tried to take a larger part in the management of her catering business? Assumed they were dating? Exclusively.

All right, those last two were probably reasonable, given they'd just slept together. Frankie wouldn't have let him near her bed unless she was confident of a future together.

Did she really just have that thought? A future with Spence? Look at the trouble she'd gotten into last time when she began making plans.

Lifting her head, she stifled a groan and punched her pillow.

"Having trouble sleeping?" Spence's low voice gave her a start.

"Sorry, I didn't mean to wake you. I was… was…" She'd rather not admit the direction her thoughts had wandered, and said the first thing to pop into her head. "The commercial smoker. Are you still willing to pick it up tomorrow?"

"I'm devoting my entire day to you and the girls."

"I'm serious, Spence."

"Me, too." He must have sensed her anxiety because he said, "Everything's going to be okay."

She flopped onto her back. "How can you be sure?"

"Don't worry. I'm not going to make unreasonable demands or invade your life."

His profile bathed in the moonlight made him look like the teenager he'd been when they first met. She recalled snuggling with him on a blanket in her dad's backyard late one night after a high school football game.

"How did you know what I was thinking?"

"You're the same Frankie Hartman you always were. And while we're on the subject, neither am I going to jump out of bed, get down on one knee and propose."

She stiffened with indignation.

"Not yet, anyway."

"I'm th—"

He didn't let her finish. "Also for the record, I'm not ruling out marriage. We'll talk when the time's right," he added.

"Spence."

"One day at a time, okay?" He pinched her chin between his thumb and index finger and tilted her face toward his.

"What about the girls? Come morning, they'll realize you've spent the night."

The chance also existed that Paige or Sienna would wake, scared from a bad dream, and come into Frankie's bedroom. What would they think when they encountered the closed door? She always left it open.

"Would you rather I leave now?" he asked.

"You'd do that?"

"Like you've always said, the girls come first. If them not finding me here is what's best, then, fine, I'll leave."

He was serious, not pulling her leg or patronizing her.

Frankie thought about her answer before giving it. "No, stay. If they ask—and who knows, they might not—we'll tell them that lots of mommies and daddies sleep together. They already have some idea from other people and watching television. If we don't make a big deal about it, they hopefully won't, either."

"Okay. We have a plan."

"Unless they say something to my family." Frankie tensed. "Paige has no filter whatsoever. I swear she loves embarrassing me."

"I say use the same strategy. Don't make a big deal out of it."

"Mel and Ronnie aren't children. They'll have a field day."

"Then tell them first, before they hear."

"Hmm." Frankie considered Spence's suggestion. "Could work if I put the right spin on it."

"What is the right spin?" He pulled her closer, turning her and fitting her into the curve of his body, her back to his broad chest.

She'd forgotten how nice that felt, being enveloped by all of him. "That we're taking things slow. Which we are. Very slow," she reiterated.

"Sure." He nuzzled her neck. "I can go slow. In fact, I'm known for my slowness."

"You don't say?" She angled her head, giving him plenty of access. "And who are these many people aware of your incredible slowness?"

"The only person I care about is you." He pressed his erection into her backside. Where had that come from? Could he possibly be ready for round two so soon?

"I think you're going to have to show me." She shifted, well aware of what his reaction would be to that subtle movement.

"Do I hear a challenge?" He reached around her, his hand delving between her legs. "Because I've never been able to refuse a challenge."

She parted her thighs so that his fingers could explore her damp folds. "Not a challenge. More of a request. Because I want you to take your time, Spence Bohanan. Make this last until you can't wait another second."

He uttered a sound, half desperation and half frustration. "You might regret those words."

Not likely. Frankie was pretty sure they were both going to drive the other one crazy. And be damn happy with the outcome.

Chapter Twelve

"You know of any other veterinarians in the area I can call besides Mel?" Spence asked Ethan.

"I have a couple names. No guarantee they'd come this far at two o'clock on a Friday afternoon. Not with the weekend looming."

The two men stood outside the stall of Spence's younger mare. The bay's head remained in the corner. She refused to face them and periodically pawed the ground.

Could be signs of colic, which wasn't good during a pregnancy. Also could be signs of uterine torsion, a serious complication that almost always required surgery. With a due date three months away, the foal's chances of survival were nonexistent.

Then again, it could be nothing. When Spence had arrived at the ranch a short time ago, he'd questioned Ethan extensively. According to him, the mare hadn't tried to lie down or roll. She'd also eaten that morning and was seen drinking water. Ethan's cursory exam had revealed nothing out of the ordinary.

Spence should be relieved, only he wasn't. Why was she standing in the corner? Even waving a carrot hadn't encouraged her to abandon her place. Had the pain in her leg flared up? The limp Mel spotted a few weeks ago seemed to have vanished. Maybe Spence should take the mare for a walk around the stables.

"Why is it you won't call Mel?" Ethan asked.

"She's pregnant. I don't want her to get hurt."

"How important is this mare and her foal to you? At least Mel could look at her."

"True."

The mare's movement was so unexpected, Spence involuntarily jerked. As if she hadn't caused the two men intense worry, she plodded to the stall door, lifted her head over and nuzzled Spence's arm.

"What's this?" He petted her nose, and she snorted in return.

Ethan stared in disbelief. "If I didn't know any better, I'd say she was pulling your leg."

The two men stayed for several more minutes, continuing to observe the mare. Spence needed to be absolutely sure she was all right.

"I heard you and Frankie are back together."

"You…what?" Spence frowned. "Who told you?"

"An educated guess. I've seen you two together around town."

He and Frankie had been attempting to keep their relationship under wraps. They were almost caught that first morning, but the girls simply assumed Spence had arrived early for breakfast. Neither did they think much about him coming over every day since.

Mel and Ronnie had probably guessed, given they were dropping hints, which Frankie chose to ignore.

Spence hadn't stayed over a second night, though he would have very much liked that. He took his cues from Frankie, and she hadn't given any indication she was ready. That wasn't to say they hadn't stolen away for a few gratifying moments alone and one very long goodbye while the girls slept.

"We're doing things together as a family," he said. "Plus she has a big catering job tomorrow that's kept her really busy. I've been helping as much as I can."

Last Sunday, they'd picked up the commercial smoker. Taking the girls, they'd made a day of it, stopping for pizza on the way home.

"But you'd like to get back together," Ethan prodded.

Spence didn't contradict his friend and instead executed a side step. "We're taking things one day at a time."

"That's what I thought."

"Hey, wait a minute."

Ethan laughed. "I've got to run. I'm meeting a client. I'll check on this girl periodically and call you if there's any indication of trouble."

"I appreciate that, pal."

No sooner had Ethan left than Spence's phone rang. "Hi, Frankie."

"Catch you at a bad time?" she asked.

"Not at all." He tried to keep the pleasure from his voice, a phenomenon that occurred each time they talked no matter how determined he was to prevent it. "What's up?"

"I hate to impose, but I need a favor."

"Hey, we're a team." He'd almost said "couple," but caught himself at the last second.

"Any chance you can drive into Scottsdale and pick up the meat at the wholesale distributor? I'm stuck at the café and can't get away."

She'd placed the order four days ago. They would have picked it up earlier, only Frankie had yet to purchase a chest freezer; Spence had deemed the one they looked at on Sunday a piece of junk. Neither of them had considered waiting to pick up the meat until today a problem.

"I thought you were scheduled to get off early."

"I was. Antonio insists I have to cover for Sherry Anne. She went home with a hundred-and-one temperature. My request for time off is personal. Antonio says because she's sick, her request trumps mine. If I refuse and clock out, he's going to write me up."

"Can he do that?"

"I don't know. And I don't have time today to be phoning the EEOC or Department of Labor or whoever one contacts to file a complaint." She called the new manager a very unflattering name under her breath. "I'd quit this stupid job if I could."

Spence held his tongue. She wouldn't let him support her and the girls until she found other employment or her catering business took off. No point in offering.

"I'll get the meat," he assured her. "Don't

worry. Just text me the distributor's name and address."

"What about Lucas? Will he mind you leaving work early?"

Spence didn't admit he'd already left, much to Lucas's consternation. He and his new boss hadn't been meshing as well as Spence had originally hoped. His fault. He'd been too optimistic. Not many horse farm owners were as amenable as Annily Farrington.

"Remember," Frankie said, "the distributor's closes at four thirty."

He checked the time on his phone. "No problem. I can make it before then."

"Can you also pick up the girls from preschool and drop them off at Mel's? She'll be done working by then and can babysit."

"I'll take them with me."

"Are you sure? Paige and Sienna can be a handful."

"They'll be fine," Spence insisted. "You've taken them to the distributor before. I can swing by the café, which is a few blocks from the preschool, and get their car seats."

"Or you can leave me your truck and take my minivan."

"Don't forget to call ahead and let the preschool know I'm coming."

"I had you added to the list of authorized people earlier this week."

She had? That as much as anything made Spence certain of her feelings for him. She trusted him with their daughters. She believed in his ability to take care of them.

With their plan coming together, they finalized a last few details before disconnecting. Spence gave the mare another quick inspection.

"Aren't you the fickle one?" He patted her neck. "Just like a female."

On the drive to the preschool, he called Mel, putting her on alert about his mare. She agreed to keep her phone close and go directly to the ranch if he called her with a problem.

Paige and Sienna were thrilled to see him when he arrived at the preschool. When they insisted they were hungry, he phoned Frankie and asked her to bring them a snack when they switched vehicles at the café. She was waiting for them outside, keys and to-go boxes in hand.

"You're the best." She gave Spence a hug, which he returned with what might be considered more than necessary enthusiasm.

"I aim to please."

She looked at him with pleading eyes. "I hate to ask, but I have another request."

He'd have given her the moon if he could.

"Will you start the smoker when you get to the house? It needs to preheat. And prep the meat. Call me and I'll talk you through the process. I already have the seasonings prepared. They're in a container on the counter. The girls can feed the pets. And there are leftovers in the fridge for dinner."

"Okay, okay. I got it." At least, he thought he did. There was a lot to remember.

They were at the edge of town when his cell phone rang yet again. "Girls, be quiet for a second. Daddy has a call and needs to hear."

When had he started referring to himself as "Daddy"?

Seeing Ethan's name on his phone display, he was immediately struck with concern. "Yeah, pal. What's up?"

"Your mare's been trying to lie down in her stall."

Not good news. And if she was experiencing uterine torsion, rolling would only worsen the condition.

"I'll be right there." Spence disconnected and immediately called Mel. When she answered, he relayed what Ethan had said. "I'm on my way," he told her. "Be there in ten minutes."

"I'm five minutes behind you," she answered.

"Where are we going?" Paige asked when he was done.

"The ranch. Daddy has a small emergency." That could actually become a large one.

All his panic and hurrying felt like an over-reaction when he arrived at Powell Ranch, to find the mare was once again behaving perfectly fine.

"Can we pet her?" Sienna crossed the invisible line Spence had instructed the twins to stand behind.

He held up a hand. "Not today, angel face. You and your sister just play for few minutes while I talk to your aunt Mel."

Sienna's pout ended the moment Paige grabbed her hand and tugged her down the aisle. Spence entered the stall. When Mel insisted on an up-close examination, he didn't object. The first thing she did was listen to the mare's side with a stethoscope.

"Sounds good," she said. "I'm hearing plenty of gut noises." After that, they walked the horse up and down the aisle. Then Mel pressed and kneaded the mare's underside. "I'm not finding any indication of pain or distress."

"What do you think I should do?"

"Just keep an eye on her. I'll stay for another hour."

"Would you? That'd be great." Spence was already planning on returning to the ranch after Frankie got home. She could pick up where he left off with smoking the brisket, ribs and chicken.

"And I'll drop by in the morning," Mel said. "Bring my X-ray equipment. I'm really leaning toward an issue with her leg."

"Are you sure?"

Rather than answer him, she asked, "Hadn't you better get going? The meat distributor is a twenty-five-mile drive."

He gave the mare a last lingering look.

"Leave, Spence. I swear I'll take good care of her."

"All right." He turned, glancing about for the twins. They were nowhere to be seen. He muttered, "Shit," and went in search of them.

They weren't in the tack room, the first place he checked; it figured they'd find a new hiding place. Five minutes later, right at the moment he was about to come unglued, he discovered them hiding behind the grain barrels.

"Come on, you two, we're running late." He took them by the hands, refusing to give in to the temper he felt brewing just beneath the surface. Paige and Sienna were kids, and he had told them to go play.

Eventually, they were on the freeway heading toward south Scottsdale. Spence let himself relax. They still had a half hour to get to the meat distributor.

Right before the Shea exit, traffic came to a grinding halt. Literally. As in a standstill. Spence swore again.

"You said a bad word," Paige admonished him from the backseat of the minivan.

"Sorry."

Five minutes later, they reached the next exit. Spence decided to travel city streets the remainder of the way and exited the freeway. But during rush hour on a Friday afternoon, those, too, were congested.

He stopped looking at the clock on the dash and tried calling Frankie. Maybe she could contact the meat distributor and let him know he was on his way. When she didn't answer, he threw his cell phone onto the passenger seat.

With no other choice, Spence drove as fast

as he dared with two youngsters in the vehicle. Every effort he made was in vain, however. When he arrived at the place, the parking lot was a ghost town and the front door locked. Repeated banging and shouting drew no one. Calling the phone number painted on the door, he got a recording.

Could this day go any worse?

He stood there, scrubbing his face, his heart sinking to the ground. He'd let Frankie down. Broken his promise to her. She was supposed to deliver enough brisket, ribs and chicken for more than three hundred guests tomorrow, and there was none.

What now?

SPENCE DIDN'T CALL FRANKIE. He should; he knew it. Even though she'd be furious with him, he had an obligation to tell her and let her decide on their next step. Rather than reach for the phone, he shoved the key in the ignition.

"Where are we going, Daddy?" Paige asked from the rear seat.

Daddy? This was the first time either twin had actually said "Daddy" and not "my daddy." Instead of being excited, he concentrated on using his phone's GPS app to locate the nearest warehouse store. No other place came to mind where he could purchase large quantities of meat.

"Bingo," he exclaimed, locating a store less than two miles away. Shifting into Drive, he headed toward the exit, the minivan rocking as they ran over a speed bump.

The girls whooped with delight and chorused, "Again."

Maybe at the warehouse store.

Because he didn't have a membership—that small detail had escaped him—he bought one. Grabbing a cart, and letting the girls push a second one, he hurriedly led the way to the meat department.

Spence had no clue what to look for when selecting brisket, ribs and chicken. Not that there was much to choose from. Grabbing cellophane-wrapped packages, he threw them into his cart, mentally tallying the pounds.

Nowhere near enough! Even with every package in the meat case, there was maybe a third of what Frankie needed. Frantically waving, he caught the attention of the butcher behind the glass window.

"Do you have any brisket back there?" he asked.

"Which cut? Flat or point?"

"Doesn't matter. I'll take whatever you have. Beef ribs, too. And whole chickens."

"Back or short ribs?"

Jeez, the guy was making this hard. "The big kind that you barbecue."

"That'd be back ribs." He ambled off.

While they waited, the girls took turns crawling underneath their cart and pushing each other around. Spence briefly considered telling them to stop, especially when an older gentleman passed them, a disapproving scowl on his face.

Spence had too much on his mind to care. He

called Ethan, who reported the mare was doing fine and that he'd check on her one last time before going home.

"Thanks, pal. I appreciate it."

The beep he'd heard during his conversation was a text arriving from Frankie. He quickly scanned the message and then promptly ignored it. He couldn't lie, and if he told her the truth, she'd start worrying. Better he wait to talk to her until he had a solution, not just a problem.

"Here you go." The butcher had brought out four more packages of brisket, ten chickens and no ribs.

"Do you have any more?"

"This is all I can sell you. Another delivery is scheduled for tomorrow afternoon, if you want to come back."

"I can't. Is there by chance a store in north Scottsdale?"

The butcher recited the location.

Paige and Sienna each wanted to push the cart with the meat. They began squabbling and continued throughout the entire checkout process. Fortunately, the cashier was speedy.

In the parking lot, Spence loaded the van as fast as humanly possible, ended the girls' bickering by putting them in their respective car seats, and zoomed off to their next stop. The routine at the second warehouse store went pretty much the same as the first, and with mostly the same results.

Taking another count, he determined there was plenty of chicken, almost enough brisket and nowhere near the amount of ribs Frankie needed. A search on his phone revealed the next nearest warehouse store was too far away. Spence decided to return home, hitting as many grocery stores as he could.

Which amounted to three. And three conversations with butchers who acted as if they couldn't care less. Eventually, Spence lost track of how much meat he'd purchased, and hoped for the best.

Frankie would have to understand. By now, she was getting off work. He sent her a text, letting her know they were on their way, but nothing else.

Not unexpectedly, she was standing out front, waiting for them, when he pulled in the driveway. The anger sparking in her eyes the last time he was late paled in comparison to tonight.

"What happened!" she demanded when he tried to explain. "Why weren't you here when I got home?"

Spence opened the rear door of the minivan and began grabbing packages, handing off the smaller ones to the girls.

"We had a little snafu."

Frankie glared at the stacks of meat. "Where did you get this? It's not from the distributor."

"By the time we arrived, the place was closed."

"How is that possible?" She stared at him as if unable to comprehend. "Did they close early?"

"I...had to stop at Powell Ranch first."

"Why?"

"My mare was sick. Don't worry—she's okay now. Mel examined her. And then there was traffic on the freeway. But first, the girls went missing at the ranch." He chuckled, attempting to lighten the mood. "It was quite the comedy of errors."

"I'm not laughing, Spence."

"I bought most of the meat at two different warehouse stores. The rest at grocery stores." After tucking packages of brisket under each arm, he carried them into the house.

Frankie did the same. Once they dumped the packages on the counter, she began meticulously inspecting each one.

"This stuff's inferior," she proclaimed. "That why I always buy from the distributor."

"I did the best I could."

"Some of the meat is frozen."

"Is it?" He hadn't noticed. Actually, he hadn't cared.

Hands braced on her hips, she faced him. "You should have called from the freeway when you realized you were going to be late. I'd have phoned the distributor and had them stay open until you got there."

"Check your phone. I did call, and you didn't answer."

"There was no voice mail message. And you didn't call again or answer my first text."

That much was true.

"Okay, okay. I messed up. Sorry." He left, returning to the minivan for another load.

She dogged his heels, telling the twins, "Go play in your room while Mommy and your daddy work." They reluctantly obeyed.

He didn't mention Paige calling him Daddy.

After carting in the last load, Frankie stood in the middle of the kitchen, surveying the mountains of packages, tears in her eyes. "I can't believe this."

"Everything's going to be fine. You're a great cook. This will be the best barbecue any of the guests have ever eaten."

"There isn't enough." A sob escaped. "And some of the meat is barely good enough to feed to the dogs."

He thought she might be exaggerating, but

refrained from commenting. He happened to like his head, and she was ready to chew it off.

"I'll do whatever you want," he said. "How can I help?"

"You're joking, of course." Her sob turned into a bitter laugh.

Again, Spence held his tongue. An outburst wouldn't benefit either of them or the situation. "I wasn't, actually."

"You cost me this catering job. What am I supposed to tell the clients? My boyfriend-slash-baby daddy-slash-business partner got delayed because his mare *might* have been sick, and he was late getting to the meat distributor?"

Did she really not understand? "Uterine torsion is a life-threatening condition. For the foal and possibly the mare. Just ask Mel."

Frankie didn't appear to have heard him. "I can't serve this meat. The chicken, maybe. Yes." She clamped a hand to her forehead. "Not the brisket or ribs. I could smoke it for two days and it'd still be tough and tasteless."

He couldn't believe every single package he'd

bought was unusable. "I get that you're mad. But is there the slightest chance you're over-reacting?"

She recoiled as if he'd uttered a horrible insult. "It's your fault we're in this situation."

"I made a mistake. I've already apologized." He removed his hat, wiped his damp brow and shoved his hat back down on his head. When he spoke again, it was through gritted teeth. "The mare. The girls running off. The traffic. You not answering your phone. Everything conspired against me."

"That's no excuse." Her movements became increasingly jerky as her aggravation increased. "You could have made any number of different decisions. Called the diner when I didn't answer. Called Mel and asked her to stop by and find me. Called the distributor when you realized you were running late."

Did she have to keep hitting him over the head with a verbal hammer?

"You asked a lot of me today."

"You assured me you could handle it. I told you to drop the girls off with Mel."

"The plan was for you to get off work early," he countered. "Had you left, we'd be loading the smoker right about now instead of arguing."

"I couldn't prevent Shelly Anne getting sick."

"And I couldn't help my very expensive pregnant mare exhibiting signs of a serious condition. But somehow, your excuse is understandable and mine isn't."

Frankie turned, fire in her eyes. "So, this is all about money? Whose business is more important?"

"That's hardly fair. Your job at the café, your livelihood, your potential future aren't on the line. If that mare and her foal had died, my chance of having my own racing horse farm would die with them."

"Well, my catering business is about to go under."

"Start over." Spence didn't see the problem. She'd hardly gotten her business off the ground.

"With what?" Frankie scoffed. "I don't have the financial resources. There's day care costs and preschool tuition, not to mention a mortgage payment, utilities, taxes and insurance."

"You might have more resources if you'd told me about the girls from the beginning and let me pay child support."

"Is this your way of extracting revenge?"

"What are you talking about?"

"You're mad at me for denying you the twins. And in exchange, you're sabotaging my business."

"How could you say that?" He almost banged the side of his head to clear his ears. Surely he hadn't heard her right. "I've let you down in the past, I won't deny that. But I never have and never will sabotage you or your business."

"I shouldn't have said that. I got carried away." Her backpedaling didn't quite ring true.

Spence breathed and silently counted to ten before saying, "I'll repeat myself. What can I do to help?"

"Nothing."

"You're giving up?"

"I have to think." Confusion and desperation marred her features. "Give me a minute."

"Should we at least start on the chicken?"

"Maybe. I don't know. What's the point if I can't smoke the brisket and ribs?"

"Frankie. Look—"

"Please." She closed her eyes and rubbed both her temples. "Maybe you should leave."

"Is that what you really want?"

She dropped her hands and stared at him. "I want my meat order."

"This isn't the end of the world."

"Don't patronize me."

"I'm at a loss, Frankie." He wasn't lying to her. "I've done the best I could to fix the problem. But it's like you didn't get what you wanted, and nothing else is acceptable."

"Now who's being unfair?"

Perhaps he *should* leave. This constant bickering was tiring and counterproductive.

"I knew better," she mumbled, her gaze roaming the piles of meat on the counter. "Yet I let myself fall into the same old trap."

"What's that? Trusting me?" he snapped.

"You have to admit this is a big screwup."

"As appealing as walking out sounds, I'm staying. Not because leaving would be admitting you're right about me. You're not. But because that would give you the excuse you need to tell yourself and everyone else I'm the same old Spence who quits when the going gets tough."

"Don't let me stop you."

A memory slammed into him. "You've said that to me before. Remember? When I took the job in Wichita."

"A job you happened to take a mere week after I brought up marriage."

"Did you ever think you drove me away?"

"That's makes no sense."

He shook his head. "I'm not the one in this relationship who's afraid of commitment, Frankie. It's you. And if I had any doubt, I need only recall that you hid our daughters from me for four years. You can't bear the thought of being stuck in a relationship with me."

Her jaw dropped open. "That's not the least bit true."

"Think about it."

"I will." She pointed to the door. "After you leave."

"All right. You win," he admitted. "I'm out of here." He grabbed his truck keys, which she'd left on the counter, moving several chicken packages to get to them. "But I'm not abandoning my daughters. If you change your mind and want me to watch the smokers, call. I'll be right over."

"I won't."

He half expected her to stop him before he reached the front door. She didn't, however, being the proud owner of a stubborn streak a mile wide. Then again, the same could be said about him. A fact that hadn't boded well for either of them in the past, nor would it in the future.

The difference was—and in Spence's mind,

it was an important one—he wouldn't skip off for parts unknown this time. He'd be back on her doorstep tomorrow, to see his daughters if nothing else.

Chapter Thirteen

Spence had messed up. Badly. Frankie reassured herself for the twentieth time she wasn't wrong for being angry at him and sending him away.

Unfortunately, by allowing her anger to rule her actions, she was now up to her elbows in meat—inferior meat at that—and with no one to help her other than two tired, cranky little girls who wanted supper and were oblivious to their mother's distress.

"Where did Daddy go?" Sienna asked, coming up behind her.

Daddy? Since when did the twins call Spence Daddy? If Frankie weren't in the middle of a crisis, she'd ponder the implications of this one small change and what caused the sharp prick in her side. Was it shock, worry…or jealousy?

Please don't let me be that petty. Not tonight.

"He had some errands to run, sweetheart."

"Were you fighting?"

"No, no." Frankie rested a hand on Sienna's shoulder. "Grown-ups talk loud sometimes. We didn't mean to upset you and your sister."

Apparently satisfied with the explanation, she said, "We're hungry."

"Right." Frankie surveyed the kitchen, hoping kid-friendly food would miraculously appear without any effort on her part. "Guess not," she muttered. Then she added in a bright voice, "Cereal and toast okay?"

Breakfast for dinner one night wouldn't hurt anyone. Frankie shoveled a bowl of fruit-flavored O's into her mouth at rapid speed and chased it with a glass of orange juice. The sugar should boost her energy enough for the next few hours.

While she ate, she considered her limited options. With most of her family out of town at the rodeo with Sam, there weren't many people available and willing to rush to her aid.

Feeling helpless and lost, she phoned her dad. Some things never changed. Just like when she was young, he was the first person she turned to in a crisis.

"Dad?" She broke into sobs. "I'm in trouble."

"Baby girl, what's wrong?"

Pulling herself together, she explained the situation, trying not to lay all the blame on Spence.

"Let me call Theo," her father said when she finished.

"What can he do?"

"The Small Change is the top cattle ranch in the valley. In this part of the state. I guarantee you, Theo has a freezer full of prime quality beef."

"I only need brisket and ribs."

"While you're waiting, go through the packages," he instructed. "Some of the meat has got to be usable. And smoking does bring out the best in even the worst cuts."

"All right." She grew marginally calmer. "I'm not sure I can prep all the meat by myself and watch the girls."

"Give me a few minutes. Try not to fret."

Frankie decided a little more than half the brisket and ribs was usable. All right, she'd overreacted, just as Spence had accused her of. She put those packages on one side of the kitchen and the rest on the other. By the time she was done, her dad phoned.

"Theo's daughter, Reese, and son-in-law, Gabe, will be there shortly with your beef. They didn't have enough. But Theo reached out to a few of the other ranchers. They all offered what they had."

"Oh, Dad." Frankie started crying again, thinking she had a lot of free catering jobs to schedule in the future. "Tell them I'll pay. I don't expect handouts."

"Reese and Gabe can't stay. But Cara and her

husband, Jake, are coming over. Pack a bag for the girls. Jake will take them home to spend the night."

"Really?"

"Cara's going to help you prep the meat, then leave. Miguel will come over when he's off work and can stay till morning."

"Miguel?" The cook from the Cowboy Up Café. "You called him?"

"He called me and offered to help. Said he and some of the other employees owe you a heap of favors. You've been taking heat from the new manager that should have been directed at them."

"I'm not sure I agree with that."

"Hey, don't look a gift horse in the mouth."

Something puzzled Frankie. "How did he know I needed help?"

"Spence told him. Guess he stopped by the café for dinner."

"Oh. That was…nice of him."

"None of my business, hon," her dad said,

"but I'm pretty sure Spence would also help if you asked."

"Probably," she agreed. "Only I'm not calling him. Not now. Tomorrow, maybe." Anything else she planned to say was delayed by the ringing of her doorbell. "Gotta go, Dad. Someone's here."

She hurried to the living room, skirting the barking dogs. For a wild second, she wondered if Spence had returned. He hadn't, of course. Why would he, after she'd pretty much thrown him out?

Plastering a smile on her face, she greeted Cara and Jake, opening the door wide to let them and their two young children inside. "I haven't had time to tell the girls yet. I'm sure they'll be thrilled."

Cara laughed. "Even though Paige is still mad at Nathan, and Kimberly threw up on her?"

"Probably shouldn't mention those things."

By making the night away sound more like a slumber party than a reason to get the twins out of the house, Frankie was able to convince them

to go along with the plan. They were just loading all the kids and toys and bags, and food containers Frankie insisted they take, when Reese
and Gabe arrived. Jake stayed to help, he and
Gabe quickly carrying in the half-dozen ice
chests containing meat.

"Love you both." Frankie waved goodbye to
the twins. "Be good." She couldn't help notic-
ing Nathan staring longingly at Paige. The little
girl didn't appear immune to him, either, though
she was being coy.

Kids. If only adult love was that simple and
the bumps as easy to overcome, Spence might
be here now.

Frankie stomped back to the kitchen, her teeth
clenched. She was mad. She was hurt. She was
incredibly overwhelmed. Thank goodness she
had until two o'clock tomorrow to deliver the
food to the family reunion. At three o'clock,
she'd allow herself the luxury of having a break-
down.

In the meantime, she had no choice but to stay
the course. This catering job was what mat-

tered the most. With the way things were going at work, or weren't going, her future could depend on it.

Kind of like Spence's racing quarter horse farm. If his mare had truly been in distress, if the foal had died, he'd have lost a sizable investment and perhaps a whole lot more.

"Are you okay?" Cara asked. She was adding water to the bucket of soaking wood chips.

"Fine." Frankie returned to prepping and seasoning the meat. "Just momentarily distracted."

Not long after that, Miguel arrived.

"The cavalry's here," she announced, letting him in.

He held up a long black carrying case. "I brought my knives. My personal set. Not those lousy ones from the café."

"You're the best." She hugged him. "I have a pile of whole chickens with your name on them. I was thinking of just cutting them in quarters."

He followed her into the kitchen, exchanged hellos with Cara and then started to work, needing very little direction.

"Why did you call my dad and not me?" Frankie asked.

"When you didn't pick up, Spence suggested I try Ray, and gave me his number."

Frankie rolled a rib in a large pan of seasoning, coating each side, and absently murmured, "I'll have to thank him."

"He could use some cheering up." Miguel quartered a whole chicken in three swift moves. "Looked down in the dumps to me. I wonder why?"

Frankie didn't answer. There was simply too much work to be done to let herself get distracted. "Anyone want some coffee? We're in for a long night."

With assembly line precision, they eventually had every piece of brisket, every rib and every chicken quarter prepped and in the smokers. At the last minute, Frankie had started her two small personal smokers, fearing there wouldn't be enough room in the commercial one. And she'd been right.

At about nine o'clock, Cara went home, taking an ice chest full of the meat Frankie had deemed not to her standards. It would be fine for home use, and she was keeping some for herself.

"I really shouldn't," Cara protested, staring at the cooler. "There has to be a couple hundred dollars' worth of meat in there."

Frankie insisted, and they lugged the ice chest to Cara's vehicle. "I owe you more than that for your and Jake's help."

She'd filled the remaining chests left by Reese and Gabe, intending to give one to Miguel and the rest to her family. While Miguel babysat the smokers, she ran to the market for bags of ice, arriving five minutes before it closed. After the reunion, when she found the time, she'd deliver the remaining chests. Until then, packed with ice, the meat would keep plenty cold.

There was also the matter of reimbursing Spence for the meat. She'd get to that, too, paying him out of the money from the client. Knowing him, he'd refuse. That wouldn't stop her from offering, however.

"Hit the sack," Miguel told Frankie. "I'll watch the smokers for a while."

"You have to be more tired than me. You worked an extra shift at the café before getting here."

"I'm fine." He was already sitting at the patio table, his feet propped on an adjacent chair. "I'll set the alarm on my phone in case I doze off."

"All right," she reluctantly agreed. "Wake me for any reason. I don't care how minor you think it is."

Every bone in Frankie's body ached, especially those in her hands and feet. Even so, she couldn't sleep. The argument with Spence played over and over in her head, refusing to let her relax. She debated texting Mel and asking about Spence's mare.

Not that she doubted him. Spence wouldn't have broken his promise to her for any trivial reason. Frankie was simply curious if the mare was doing okay.

Well, that wasn't entirely true. As much as she wanted to believe Spence, doubts plagued her.

Why hadn't he called, dammit? Kept calling when he didn't initially reach her? Then none of this would have happened. They'd have prepared the meat together, and he'd be on the patio instead of Miguel. Or here, in her bed, making love to her while the smokers toiled.

His lack of consideration was what really angered her. Spence thought solely of himself. He'd never put his family first. Put her first. She'd been right to send him away and would be a fool to consider taking him back for even one second.

That didn't stop her heart from breaking clean in half.

He'd been wrong when he'd accused her of fearing commitment. Frankie loved Spence. She always had. If not, she wouldn't be lying with her face buried in her pillow now, crying until no more tears remained.

"THANKS, LUCAS." SPENCE shook hands with the racing quarter horse owner. "I appreciate the offer more than you know."

"You're a good trainer. With the potential to be a great one."

Spence shrugged off the compliment. "I still have a lot to learn."

He'd been in Florence since early morning, working with the colt—as much to avoid thinking of his and Frankie's blowup as making a final decision on whether or not working with Lucas was the best career decision for him.

"I'd sure like to be the one to help teach you," Lucas said.

His offer had been a generous one that included accommodations for Spence's two mares and any other horses he might buy, along with the foals they produced.

"And I couldn't ask for a better mentor." Spence shook the other man's hand before getting in his truck.

During the hour drive home to Mustang Valley, he mentally reviewed his options. The best choice was probably taking Lucas's offer and moving to Florence. Only, he'd declined. Something about the job didn't feel right. Though the colt showed promise, he hadn't lit a spark inside Spence, not like Han Dover Fist did the first time Spence saw the horse run. He'd known in an instant his fate was tied to the big, handsome horse, and he'd been right.

Mostly, his reservations stemmed from working for someone else with no chance of ownership whatsoever. That wasn't acceptable. If Spence had learned one thing about himself these past few years, it was he needed to be his own boss. He hadn't hopped from one job, one town, to another because of any wanderlust.

Rather, he'd been searching. For something else, something better, something that would allow him to be the captain of his own ship.

Okay, that sounded corny, but it was true. Maybe like his father, Spence had a compelling drive to make it on his own. Be the one to take all the credit for his success and, like it or not, all the blame. Was that so bad?

He could always move back to Marana. His family would certainly welcome him with open arms. Except that felt too much like going backward instead of forward.

There was also nothing stopping him from returning to Cottonwood Farms in California. He did have that open invitation from his former boss, and he'd be able to take his mares.

Except he'd be separated from Paige and Sienna by hundreds of miles. Whatever direction Spence took, wherever he wound up, it would be close to his daughters. He'd made a commitment to them and Frankie, and Spence was a man who kept his word. Granted, at one time that hadn't been true. Frankie would no doubt agree. But he truly was a different man these days.

If not in Mustang Valley, then Spence would live and work at a place near enough to see the girls often, help Frankie to raise them, and eventually share custody. The fact that he still cared for Frankie with every fiber of his being shouldn't factor into his decision, though it did. He refused to venture far from her, too.

As he stopped for gas at the station on the

edge of town, he began having second thoughts. His money, which had once seemed abundant, was disappearing fast. He'd shelled out a fair amount already for child support, rental on the mares' stalls, vet bills and Frankie's catering business.

Lucas gave him a check today, but it was only enough to pay Eddie for use of his spare bedroom these past weeks, with a little left over for groceries.

If he was going to prove his claims of having matured in recent years were founded, he'd have to develop a plan of action quick before his money ran out.

He debated calling Frankie and checking on how she'd fared with the catering job, but resisted. Instead, he drove to the local bank, which was open for another twenty minutes, intending to cash his check.

While waiting for the teller to finish with the customer ahead of him, Spence glanced at the posters offering various services. An idea sprang into his head and quickly took shape.

Stepping up to the counter, he said, "Hi. I'd like to open an account."

"Certainly, sir." The young man smiled. "The assistant manager will be right with you."

The assistant manager turned out to be Reese Dempsey, daughter of Theo McGraw, who owned The Small Change Ranch.

"How are you?" She greeted him warmly and led him to her office with its large glass window looking out to the bank lobby.

"Real good. Tell your dad hello for me."

"I will. He's quite fond of you." She sat at her desk while Spence lowered himself into the visitor chair.

"The feeling's mutual."

"He was very impressed with your mock race and all the money donated for the sanctuary."

"Couldn't have done it without him."

"Gabe and I saw Frankie just last night. We took her over a bunch of beef for her catering job. She tell you?"

"No." Spence tried not to show his surprise.

"Oops." Reese's cheeks colored slightly. "Sorry. I figured…my mistake."

"Hey, no problem. I'm glad you helped her." He should have counted on Frankie finding a creative solution for the catastrophe he'd caused.

"What kind of account are you looking to open?" Reese asked, smoothly bringing their discussion around to the reason for his visit.

"Come to think of it, I might need two accounts. A checking and a joint savings. Is something like that possible?"

"Absolutely," Reese assured him, beaming. Swiveling her computer monitor so Spence could see the display, she started typing on the keyboard. "We have several products available."

Opening two accounts took them well past closing time. Reese didn't appear to be in a hurry. One of the benefits of small-town living, Spence supposed. People weren't just customers, they were friends and neighbors.

Feeling better and better about this inspired step he'd taken, Spence bade Reese goodbye and left the bank. As if a door had been opened, another idea came to him. It was almost too crazy to consider. Luckily, Spence was a risk taker.

Sitting behind the steering wheel, he dug in his wallet for the business card Annily Farrington had given him at the adoption event. Finding it at last, he stared at her phone number, address and racing farm logo while remembering their recent conversation.

"I briefly considered finding a new business partner, then decided I'd try downsizing first. I've never been the easiest person to get along with. Hate to put that burden on someone I like."

He'd meant to call her, but his mind had been otherwise occupied these past two weeks. Well, as the old saying went, no time like the present.

When she didn't answer, he left a voice mail message. She called back before he reached the next stop sign.

"Sorry I missed you," she said brightly. "I was on the treadmill. Doctor claims if I don't exercise every day, I'll be in a wheelchair within a year. What does he know?"

Same as before, Spence didn't press for information regarding her health, though being in a wheelchair did sound serious. Annily was a fighter, however, and he didn't see her giving up easily.

After a brief round of small talk, Spence asked, "Any chance you're free this afternoon?"

"You wanting to bring those girls of yours out for a visit?"

"I do, but not today. There's something else I'd like to run by you, if you have the time."

"Now I'm curious. Everything's okay?"

"Hopefully better than okay." Or, more likely, he'd had a harebrained scheme and she'd laugh in his face. "I can be there in a half hour."

"Perfect. I just made a jug of sun tea. See you then."

He stopped at the market on his way out of town for a couple chocolate bars—Annily favored the caramel-filled ones. Yes, he was attempting to butter her up before springing his idea on her. Why lie?

Annily threw open the front door before he'd even shut off his engine. Doing her best to hide a limp, she showed him to her large, comfortable country kitchen. She didn't believe in living rooms, preferring the kitchen for entertaining and socializing. A pitcher of iced sun tea and two glasses were already set out on the table.

After Spence caught her up on the latest and showed her pictures of the twins on his phone, she came right to the point. "Which do you want to do first? Tour the farm or talk business? 'Course, I'm guessing whatever you want to run by me is business, seeing as you didn't bring the girls."

Annily might be getting older, but she was sharp as ever. Spence chuckled and shook his head in amusement. "Any reason we can't do both at the same time?"

"Not at all." She pushed herself to her feet, needing to brace a hand on the table for extra support.

Outside the back door was an electric-oper-ated golf cart. She slid into driver's seat and started the engine.

"We can cover more ground faster this way," she said, and off they went.

Farrington Farms was a third the size of Annily's former place. Even so, she'd spared no expense. Every piece of equipment was brand-new and of the highest quality or latest technol-ogy. The stalls in the horse stable were roomy, well ventilated and freshly cleaned. As they traveled the stable aisle, he admired her excep-tional racing stock. Annily filled him in on the horses' various pedigrees. Spence recognized most of the lines.

The well-manicured practice track circled a large oval grassy area. In the center, flower boxes overflowing with colorful pansies were lined up in a long row. Two feed barns were filled with the finest quality alfalfa and grains. Three outbuildings sat clustered between the pastures and the race track.

"You have a beautiful place here, Annily." Spence couldn't be more sincere in his praise.

"I thought by downsizing, I'd be able to stay in the race game. Not sure I can if I'm in a wheelchair." She grumbled with disgust. "Sucks getting old. Sucks more having osteoporosis."

Spence suspected there might be more going on healthwise. She'd become very short of breath when they were touring the practice track.

"What if I could help you?" he asked.

Interest flared in her eyes. "You looking for a job?"

They walked slowly from the outbuildings to where Annily had parked the golf cart, and then stopped in the shade to continue their conversation.

"Yes and no," Spence said. "What I'd like is to be your partner."

"You don't say?" She narrowed her gaze. "And how do you envision this partnership working?"

Okay, she hadn't laughed in his face or thrown him out on his hind end. That was encouraging.

"I'd need a job, yes. That's a fact. And a place for my mares and their foals. I was thinking a portion of each of my paychecks could go toward buying a small share of Farrington Farms. I also have some cash I can put down, as well. I realize none of this will happen overnight. You have a fine place worth a lot of money."

"The property itself would have to remain mine and separate from the partnership. Anything happens to me, it goes to my daughter."

"Naturally."

She named an amount. "That's what my accountant tells me the actual racing operation is worth, including my horses."

Spence whistled. It was a hefty sum.

"We can take the horses out of the deal," she suggested.

"I have no problem with that."

Annily scrutinized Spence for so long, he started sweating around the collar. Finally, she broke the silence. "Would you consider giving me half ownership of whichever foal I choose?"

"Yes."

"And half ownership of any foal that comes from breeding your mares to my stud?"

Again, Spence agreed. "Absolutely."

"I have a trainer already."

"It's not my intention to take his job."

Her loud, sharp cackle dissolved into a cough. "Like hell it isn't."

"Not right away," Spence amended.

"You can start out as assistant trainer and barn manager. From there, we'll see how it goes."

"I accept."

"Good. I'll contact my attorney on Monday." They shook hands, after which Annily motioned for him to accompany her to the golf cart. "You planning on commuting every day from Mustang Valley?"

"If I have to. I'd rather find something closer and with enough room I can bring my girls for the weekend."

"I may have a solution."

"What's that?"

"You just be patient."

She drove them to the main house, then around

the back along a side road paved with cobble-stones. Spence's confusion cleared when an adobe casita came into view.

"This is a guesthouse for my kids and grand-kids when they visit. Which, now that my daughter's moved to Florida, won't be all that often." She twisted in her seat to face him. "I reckon it'd make a nice place for you and your girls. Temporarily, anyway. Until you find more permanent digs. I'll include the rent as part of your salary."

Spence didn't consider himself an emotional man, but in that moment, he felt his throat close.

"I can't thank you enough, Annily."

"All I ask is that you don't disappoint me."

He started to say, "I won't," then stopped himself. He'd made that same promise to Frankie, and yet somehow he'd let her down more than he'd dreamed possible.

"I'll do my best," he finally said.

Chapter Fourteen

Frankie hastily turned as Spence entered the kitchen. Schooling her features into a congenial mask, she willed her breathing to slow to a rate resembling normal.

When the doorbell first rang, the girls had raced each other, dead set on being the one to let him in. Frankie had ignored the arguing, letting Paige and Sienna settle this one between themselves. She wasn't up to it, mentally or physically—and certainly not emotionally.

In the last two weeks since her and Spence's breakup, falling out, parting of the ways, conscious uncoupling—whatever they'd once had and didn't have now—Frankie had been miserable.

Really! It wasn't as if she loved him. Not like before. Then, she'd—

Oh, forget it.

"Hi." He grinned. "How's it going?"

"Fine." She leaned a hip on the counter.

"What's new?"

"Not much."

She'd be surprised if anything new had happened in the hour since they'd last spoken on the phone, finalizing the details of the twins' first overnight stay with him. Or since yesterday, when she'd driven out to Farrington Farms to see the casita prior to giving her consent for the overnight.

In addition to talking once or twice daily, in person or on the phone, Spence had been picking up the girls from preschool twice each week and taking them to dinner. This week, his parents and his brother's family drove up from Marana to join them. Paige and Sienna hadn't stopped talking about their younger cousins and the kid-friendly restaurant they'd eaten at, with games and rides.

Always, Frankie and Spence's conversations were about the girls or something related to them. Nothing personal. Certainly nothing intimate or remotely hinting at intimate. Not a single, solitary comment had been made about the night they'd spent together.

"Are you packed yet?" Spence asked.

"Almost," Paige reported.

"Do you have your sleeping bags?"

"We slept in them last night." Sienna glanced worriedly at Frankie. "Mommy said it was okay."

"On top of their beds." Frankie lifted one shoulder. "You don't mind?"

"'Course not."

Spence had taken the girls to a discount store in Scottsdale and purchased child sleeping bags. The idea was Frankie's. His casita at Farrington Farms had only one bedroom, but a Murphy bed pulled down from the living room wall, perfect for two little girls. Sleeping bags would be far more convenient than blankets and sheets, and a lot more fun.

"All right. Let's finish packing." Frankie started to accompany the twins.

"No, Mommy," Paige insisted. "We can do it ourselves."

Frankie met Spence's mostly unreadable gaze. He was really good at keeping his feelings to himself. "Who knows what they'll have in their backpacks when they get there."

"It's one night. We'll survive."

He was right.

"Can I get you a cold drink while you wait?"

"I'm fine, thanks." He pulled out a chair from the table. "Mind if I sit? Twisted my ankle yesterday."

She hadn't noticed him favoring a leg. But then, she'd purposely avoided gawking at him, afraid he might catch her. "Have an accident working with the horses?"

"I wish that was my excuse. Actually, I was on Annily's treadmill."

"What?" Frankie couldn't help herself and laughed. "You're exercising?" He had to be the fittest person she knew. What use would he have for a treadmill?

"The darn thing broke down, and she asked if I could fix it for her."

"And after you did, you tested it out?"

"Something like that."

Their conversation was relaxed and friendly. Too friendly. As if they were trying really hard to prove they could get along.

Did he also regret what had happened between them? Hard to tell; he seemed to be coping well.

"Other than that, how's the job going?" she asked.

"Great. Not a single complaint."

She'd been impressed with Spence when he informed her of his job/partnership agreement with Annily Farrington. He'd returned to Mustang Valley to start his own racing quarter horse farm and was well on his way. Perhaps not how he'd first envisioned his plan materializing, but it was materializing nonetheless.

Her plan, not so much. She'd done one small job since the family reunion. A dinner party with twenty guests. And not a single phone inquiry since. All that money spent on a commercial smoker, printing flyers, the many favors she owed family and friends, her falling out with Spence, had ultimately been for nothing. I-Hart-Catering was a dud.

How had Spence, a notorious flake, succeeded in realizing his goals and not her? Okay, he wasn't a flake. Not entirely. But she was the one who'd worked her tail off for years, and he got lucky betting on horses.

Also not fair, Frankie chided herself. Time to stop with the personal pity party.

Spence gave her a once-over. Apparently he'd noticed she wasn't wearing her uniform, because he asked, "Weren't you scheduled to work today?"

"Originally. I switched days with Sherry Anne and am taking the afternoon off."

"Good. You deserve a break."

At that moment, the twins came out from their

bedroom, lugging their backpacks and carrying enough toys for a week rather than one night.

Frankie walked them outside, where they switched the car seats from her minivan to his truck.

"Bye, Mommy," the girls chorused from the backseat.

"Don't give your dad any trouble."

"We won't."

Frankie backed away from the truck. Without warning, Spence's arm snaked out and grabbed her waist, startling her. "Wha—"

"Thank you." He pulled her into a hug and held on. "This means a lot to me. You trusting me with the girls."

"Sure."

He smelled incredible. She tried not to breathe, but then he tightened his hold on her, and she inadvertently inhaled. Mmmm—

Stop!

The pathetic attempt she made to extricate herself resulted in her mouth making brief contact with his jaw.

He emitted a low sound of pleasure.

Fan-freakin-tastic. Now he probably thought she'd kissed him on purpose. This was going from bad to worse.

"Spence." Escaping his hold, she retreated a step.

"We'll call you when we get there."

"Yes. Please."

He acted as if they hadn't been clinging to each other mere seconds earlier.

Then again, maybe they hadn't, and her imagination was playing tricks on her. That was a possibility. Right before Spence arrived, she had been bemoaning her miserable and lonely existence.

Smiling and waving, she waited until the truck reached the corner before going inside. The long afternoon, evening and all of tomorrow morning stretched ahead, with nothing interesting to occupy her other than housework and dwelling on recent regrets.

She was tossing another load of laundry into the washer when her cell phone chimed. Not recognizing the number, she let the call go to voice mail. Almost immediately, her curiosity got the best of her, and she listened to the message.

"Hi, Frankie. This is Marilyn Thompson. I was at the adoption event and got one of your flyers. Can you please give me a call at your earliest convenience? I'd love to chat with you about catering our wedding reception."

Frankie couldn't dial the woman's number fast enough. "Hello, Marilyn?"

The bride-to-be babbled excitedly about the cowboy-themed wedding she and her groom were planning. They'd wanted to elope, and then leave for a week-long honeymoon in Cabo San Lucas, but both their families had raised such a fuss, they'd decided on a spur-of-the-moment wedding.

"We fly out Saturday morning," Marilyn said. "A judge is marrying us at my parents' home Friday afternoon and we were hoping you could cater a reception dinner. We're skipping the white dress and tux and wearing jeans and cowboy hats instead. Won't that be cute?"

"I love it!"

This was exactly the big distraction Frankie needed. "How many guests?"

"About seventy. Our parents are going overboard."

They discussed the menu. Marilyn was happy to keep things simple. She wanted several sides to go with the brisket and chicken, including beans, coleslaw and homemade biscuits. Frankie told her she'd call back in an hour with a quote.

"You're the best," Marilyn said, a smile in her voice.

Just planning the menu and figuring the price put Frankie in a better mood. What was the old saying about happiness being contagious?

Marilyn was delighted with the price. "And can you also supply tables and chairs, and dinnerware and linens?"

"Certainly." Frankie jotted down a note to hire help.

She and Marilyn agreed on a time later in

the week to meet at Marilyn's mother's house, where Frankie would inspect the premises and have Marilyn sign a contract. With that done, she called the party rental store to place her order, which also included chafing dishes.

"We'll need a deposit," the woman said. "We take credit cards by phone."

"Sure. Hold on." Frankie retrieved her purse. Unsure how much remained on her credit line, she worried if the charge would go through. Thankfully, it did.

When she called the meat distributor, they also requested a deposit.

"Is this a new policy?" Frankie asked. "I've never had to put down a deposit before."

"Well," the owner drawled. "That was before you placed an order and didn't pick it up."

She gritted her teeth. Yet another repercussion from Spence's monstrous whoops. "I can mail you a check tomorrow." She'd move heaven and earth if necessary to find the money.

"We take credit cards," the man said.

Of course they did.

The Fates had to be smiling on Frankie, for that charge also went through. A quick phone call afterward revealed she had less than thirty dollars available on her account.

Where was she going to get the money to fund Marilyn's wedding reception? Frankie didn't usually run this close on her expenses, but she'd just paid property taxes and the quarterly preschool tuition bill, both of which had gone up several hundred dollars.

She certainly wasn't asking Spence. No way. She started to pull up her crowd-funding campaign on her phone, only to remember she'd closed it down two weeks ago, figuring she didn't need it. Shoot!

Her parents would lend her the money, but she hated asking them, even though the loan would be short-term. Her father had been very generous with her recently, sharing his lottery winnings so that she could buy her house. Requesting more made her feel greedy and unappreciative.

No, she was going to resolve this problem on

her own. She'd go to the bank and get a small loan against the equity in her house. That was what people did, right?

Lucky for her, the girls were with Spence. They'd never sit still while Frankie completed the loan paperwork. After throwing on semi-nice clothes, she hopped in her minivan and headed to the bank. After a five-minute wait, Reese Dempsey came out from her office to fetch her.

"I'm glad you're here," Reese said warmly.

"You are?" Frankie followed the other woman into her office.

"I've had the signature cards sitting on my desk for two weeks."

She sat down in the nearest chair. "Is my other card outdated or something?" She must have received a notice in the mail and accidentally thrown it away.

"No. For the new account." Reese's smile never wavered as she pushed papers across the desk toward Frankie.

"What new account?"

"Sorry." Reese looked confused. "Spence said he'd tell you and have you come in."

"Spence?" Frankie knitted her brow. It was her turn to look confused.

"He opened an account for the girls and added you as a signatory. Their college fund, he said."

Frankie was momentarily struck speechless. Spence had started a college fund for Paige and Sienna? "How much is in it?"

"Twenty thousand dollars."

"You're kidding!"

Reese stared at her curiously. "That's not why you came in today?"

"I had no idea." When had he planned on telling her? "I was going to talk to you about a home equity loan."

"Well, we can certainly arrange that, too. But in the meantime, you'd make my job easier if you'd sign these." She held out a pen.

Frankie hesitated, reading the account information. Twenty thousand dollars was no small sum and represented a good portion of Spence's money. Money he could have used to purchase a larger partnership share of Farrington Farms. Only he hadn't. Instead, he'd thought first of the twins and their future education.

Could she have been wrong about him? Blinded by her anger? He had tried to solve the problem when he'd arrived late to the distributor, even if half the meat he'd purchased wasn't good enough quality.

What if he hadn't called her because he knew she'd react exactly the way she did? Namely, get mad, blame him and refuse to listen to his side of the story?

A soft groan escaped her as understanding dawned. While Spence had been responsible and thoughtful, caring and selfless, she'd been angry, intolerant and unforgiving.

Frankie dropped her head into her hand.

"Is something wrong?" Reese asked.

"Nothing I can't fix." Flooded with determination and remorse, she scratched her signature on the papers, grabbed her purse and stood. "Thanks for your help, Reese."

"What about the home equity loan?"

"I'll be back tomorrow. I have something more important to take care of first."

"YOU'RE OLD!" Paige exclaimed.

Spence was a fairly easygoing person. Not the type to become flustered or embarrassed easily. Yet his twin daughters had succeeded where others dismally failed. Succeeded three times since he'd brought them to Farrington Farms, what? Two hours ago?

First, Sienna had accidentally stepped in a pile of horse manure outside the stables and screamed as if her hair were on fire. The head trainer and a barn hand had come running, the trainer holding out his phone, ready to dial 911.

When Spence took her over to the hose bib and rinsed off her sneakers, she'd sobbed hysterically, demanding to change into different shoes. And when Annily had been kind enough to bring out an old pair of rubber boots, Sienna pitched a fit, claiming, "They're ugly and they stink."

It appeared Spence might be making a trip to

Scottsdale tonight for new shoes. At least the twins liked the pull-down Murphy bed in the casita, declaring it "Cool."

Now, Paige stood with her hands on her hips—her resemblance to Frankie downright uncanny—and giving Annily careful consideration.

Before Spence could apologize to his boss for the rude remark, she erupted in a loud belly laugh.

"You're right about that, cuddle bug. I am old."

"Paige," Spence said, "please apologize to Mrs. Farrington."

"For what?" the little girl asked, her mouth compressed into a pout.

"Saying someone's old isn't polite."

"Why?"

Sienna had turned away and was staring at the house, ignoring them while she continued to sulk over the shoe disaster.

"People shouldn't comment on a person's age," Spence tried to explain. The more time he spent with his daughters, the more trouble he had getting them to understand what made perfect sense to him.

"Don't worry yourself about it." Annily patted Paige's head. "I'm not insulted."

Spence had started to think the overnight visit was a bad idea. How could he have thought parenting was easy? It was without question the most difficult job he'd ever attempted.

His respect for Frankie grew yet again. She'd done amazingly well, all by herself. And rather than help her or simplify her life, he'd caused her trouble with one mistake after the other.

"It's Mommy!" Sienna's high-pitched voice threatened to rupture Spence's eardrums, and she started to run.

He caught her before she got more than a few feet away. "Wait. Don't take off."

"But she's here." Sienna pulled against his hold.

Indeed, Frankie's minivan drove slowly through the gate. She stopped, perhaps to get her bearings, then started forward again. Spotting them in front of the stables, she waved.

"Mommy!" Paige jumped up and down with excitement.

What was she doing here?

Annily stepped up beside him. "Did you forget something?"

"Apparently so." *That must be the reason,* thought Spence. "I can only hope she brought a pair of shoes for Sienna."

He motioned for Frankie to park near the hitching rail, and taking the girls' hands, walked over to meet her. Annily came, too.

"You're here!" Sienna shouted.

There was no stopping the twins once Frankie stepped out of the van. They freed themselves from Spence and charged her, clinging to her for dear life.

Spence grumbled under his breath. The last couple hours weren't *that* bad.

"Hi." Annily extended her hand to Frankie. "Welcome, and nice to meet you. Sorry I wasn't here yesterday when you dropped by."

Frankie surveyed her surroundings. "Your place is gorgeous. What amazing views."

"Thank you. I'm very proud of Farrington Farms."

"We petted the horses," Paige announced.

"How nice." Frankie gave each girl a squeeze.

"Sienna stepped in poop and cried."

"Uh-oh."

Sienna buried her face in Frankie's leg.

"What brings you here?" Spence asked. Had her mom instinct reached across the miles, alerting her that the girls weren't happy?

"I apologize for barging in without calling ahead, but I need to talk to you." She shifted uncomfortably. "It couldn't wait until tomorrow."

"Okay."

She'd changed her mind and had come to retrieve the girls. What other explanation could there be than she didn't trust him, after all?

Well, he'd fight her, he decided. She couldn't just show up out of the blue and disrupt their plans, no matter how angry she was at him.

Fidgeting, she pushed at her short hair. "Wow.

I practiced what I was going to say on the drive here, and now I can't remember a single word."

"I have an idea." Annily bent and lowered her face to the girls' level. "Why don't you two come with me inside the house? Give your folks a few minutes alone to talk. I have some home-made brownies, if your mom says it's okay, and a jump rope in the closet that belongs to my granddaughter."

Sienna frowned and shook her head.

Paige, however, showed interest. "I want a brownie."

"Mommy won't be long." Frankie gave them a little shove toward Annily.

Once they left, Frankie continued to push at her hair and fidget.

Her nervousness started wearing off on Spence. "What's wrong?"

"Nothing. I—" She surprised him by reaching for his hand. "Walk with me."

He recalled the night they'd told the girls he was their father. She'd impulsively held his hand then, too, for support. What was her reason now?

"I was at the bank today," she finally said. "I wanted to get a line of credit against the equity in my house. For a big catering job."

"You need money? Why didn't you ask me?"

"I was trying to resolve the problem on my own."

"I understand."

"I know you do," she said. "Took me a while, but I see you really were trying to fix things when the distributor was closed. I'm sorry for not listening and not appreciating your efforts."

"Um, thanks?" Not at all where he'd expected their conversation to go. "You were right, though. I should have contacted you instead of going straight to the stores."

"We're the same in that regard. Both problem solvers."

The pressure of her fingers increased, and Spence experienced the many effects. He could barely draw a decent breath. Swore his heart might explode. Battled a wild desire to stop short and haul her flush against him.

Perhaps he should dial back that last one.

"We're also the same when it comes to business," she continued, seemingly oblivious to his inner turmoil. "We're ambitious and want to be our own boss."

"I think that's why I never settled down before."

"So do I," she agreed.

"In case you're worried, don't be. I'm staying, Frankie. For good. You can take that to the bank."

She stopped and faced him but didn't let go of his hand. "Speaking of the bank, Reese mentioned the college fund you opened for the girls."

"She's not very good at keeping secrets."

"Why didn't you tell me?"

"I figured you'd get mad and insist I close the account."

The hint of a smile lit her face. "Kind of stubborn, aren't I?"

"I prefer 'independent.'"

"You could have used that money to buy a larger partnership share of Farrington Farms. But you put the girls first. Nothing you've done has impressed me more, Spence."

"Yeah, well, you have every reason not to trust me. To hate me, if you chose."

Her expression softened. "That would be impossible."

He went still. Something had definitely changed with her, but he couldn't put his finger on it.

"Why, Frankie?" Excitement surged inside him, and he moved closer.

She did, too. "I love you, Spence. I always have and always will. You drive me crazy. Infuriate me to the point I want to scream." She lifted her arms and linked them around his neck. "You're also the sweetest, funniest, most charming and sexiest man I know. You work as hard as you play and love even harder. You make me feel like there's nobody else in the world you'd rather be with."

"There isn't. I came back to Mustang Valley with one purpose in mind. Winning you back." When had his voice gone hoarse? "The funny thing is I found a whole lot more. I found a family."

"One you weren't ready for."

"No." He anchored her to him. "You're wrong about that. I love those girls. They're everything to me."

"That's good." She angled her body, fitting herself to him as if they were two halves of a whole. "Because they're everything to me, too."

"See? One more thing we have in common."

She laughed, the sound light and carefree and full of delight. The way it should be between two people who were—yes, he could say it—meant to be together.

"I want to be more than your business partner," Spence said.

"Is that a proposal? Because before you answer, I landed a catering job this weekend and need some cheap labor."

"Where do I apply?"

"Are you sure? The interview process is very extensive." Her arms tightened, and she lifted her mouth within kissing range. "It might take several hours and require your undivided attention."

"I'll clear my schedule." Brushing his lips across hers, he said, "Now, about that proposal."

"Don't rush me. I'm thinking." She smiled coyly. "I've been waiting a lot of years for this moment and am going to savor it."

"Then allow me do a better job." Spence captured her gaze. "Marry me, Frankie Hartman. Not because it's the right thing to do, though it is. Not because you, me and the girls deserve to be a family, which we do. And not because you and I would make good business partners, once you whip me into shape."

"Spence." Her expression melted.

"I love you, honey. And if you just say yes, we can have it all. Our daughters, your catering business, my racing farm."

"Whoa, cowboy. You're sweeping me off my feet."

"I'm saving that for later. Now, pick a date."

She laughed again. "Let's talk about it. There's still my job at the café. I either commit to the change in management and do my best, or I leave."

"I'll support you whatever you decide."

"That means a lot to me."

He kissed her then, hard and long and without holding back. Emotions arched between them, old as the day they'd first met and new as tomorrow's sunrise. They would, Spence had no doubts, be there always.

"Mommy. Daddy! What are you doing?" Paige and Sienna's voices carried across the distance.

Slowly, Spence and Frankie broke apart.

"I suppose we'll have to get used to being interrupted."

"You mind?" she asked, just as the twins reached them.

"Not at all."

For now, Spence was reveling in his family. Life had certainly thrown him some incredible twists and turns lately—ultimately landing him right where he was supposed to be. Personally, he couldn't wait for what came next.

* * * * *

MILLS & BOON®
Hardback – August 2017

ROMANCE

An Heir Made in the Marriage Bed	Anne Mather
The Prince's Stolen Virgin	Maisey Yates
Protecting His Defiant Innocent	Michelle Smart
Pregnant at Acosta's Demand	Maya Blake
The Secret He Must Claim	Chantelle Shaw
Carrying the Spaniard's Child	Jennie Lucas
A Ring for the Greek's Baby	Melanie Milburne
Bought for the Billionaire's Revenge	Clare Connelly
The Runaway Bride and the Billionaire	Kate Hardy
The Boss's Fake Fiancée	Susan Meier
The Millionaire's Redemption	Therese Beharrie
Captivated by the Enigmatic Tycoon	Bella Bucannon
Tempted by the Bridesmaid	Annie O'Neil
Claiming His Pregnant Princess	Annie O'Neil
A Miracle for the Baby Doctor	Meredith Webber
Stolen Kisses with Her Boss	Susan Carlisle
Encounter with a Commanding Officer	Charlotte Hawkes
Rebel Doc on Her Doorstep	Lucy Ryder
The CEO's Nanny Affair	Joss Wood
Tempted by the Wrong Twin	Rachel Bailey

0717 GEN STD HB